Trying to Love

By QuanTina Gill

Copyright

Trying to Love

Copyright © 2022 Quantina Gill

All Rights Reserved

Contents

Copyright..2

Chapter 1 1

Chapter 2 8

Chapter 3 16

Chapter 4 23

Chapter 5 31

Chapter 6 38

Chapter 7 48

Chapter 8 56

Chapter 9 65

Chapter 10 74

Chapter 11 83

Chapter 12 90

Chapter 13 98

Chapter 14 105

Chapter 15 115

Chapter 16 124

Chapter 17 134

Chapter 18 139

Chapter 19 151

Chapter 20 160

Chapter 21 168

Chapter 22 177

Chapter 23 184

Chapter 24 190

Chapter 25 197

Chapter 26 204

Chapter 27 212

Chapter 28 220

Chapter 29 229

Chapter 30 234

Message from the author 242

Chapter 1

Waking up with sweat all over my body and shaking like something just scared me out of my sleep. Well, something did scare me out of my sleep, the nightmare I have been having ever since I can remember.

A nightmare I can never tell anyone about. A nightmare that will haunt me for the rest of my life, because of this nightmare I can never trust again. I can never hold a relationship because I'm scared of being touched.

Since I know I can't go back to sleep I got up and took a quick shower to get started with my day.

After I was done getting ready, I went downstairs and made myself some breakfast before it was time for me to head out for school.

While I'm sitting here eating, I will introduce myself. I'm London Wilson, I'm 23 years old. I'm a college student. I'm in school to become an English teacher, this is my last year of school and I'll officially be a high school English teacher. I have been living on my own since I was 17 years old.

Once I was done with my breakfast, I wash the dishes and grabbed my bag and keys heading out the door. After making sure everything was locked up, I got into my car and headed to school.

It's only 8:30 AM and my first class doesn't start until 9:30 AM, so I'm an hour early but I'm fine with that because it will give me more time to go over some more work for English class.

I was deep in my work that I didn't notice someone had sat down across from me and cleared their throat. I wanted to act as if they didn't just scare the shit out of me. I looked up and glared at the person that sat down.

"Don't be giving me that look, I've been calling your name since I came up to the table." My best friend said while glaring back at me.

"Erica, I didn't hear you. I was busy going over some work for Professor Smith's class, you know how she can be if our work is not done." She nodded her head, and I went back to looking over my essay we had to turn in today.

"Yeah, she can be a real bitch sometimes, but I still love her more than the other Professors." I will have to agree with her there because everyone else that works at this school is a real bitch and doesn't truly care about the students they're teaching.

I looked at the time and saw that I had 15 minutes left to get to her class, I packed up my things and started walking toward class with Erica following beside me.

Erica and I have been friends since we were in high school together. We promised each other that we will try to get into the same school, which we did, and I was super happy about it because she is my only true friend and knows about everything that has happened in my life.

We walked into the class and saw a few students there that were on time which honestly surprised me because no one is ever here before me. They must be trying to suck up to the Professor. It was a lot of people that tried to suck up to Professor Smith when they are late too many times or when their grade is dropping.

I'm lucky I don't ever be late and that my work is always on time, I'm also the best student in my class. I know because she tells the class all the time, they need to be more like me and be on time and put more effort into their work.

I sat in my seat a few chairs away from her desk and Erica sat next to me. "Why do you always sit up close like this?" She leaned over and asked me.

"I want to make sure I get everything down to pass the class with a high A." I simply said while going into my bag and taking out my essay and my notebook for the class.

"Good morning class, I hope everyone did their essay and is ready to turn it in." A lot of people groan, and some just nodded their heads.

She had us pass our essays up to the front and told us she would have them back to us with a comment by next week.

I was a little worried about this essay because I was not able to focus much on it due to the nightmares I've been having and coming home late from work.

You would think I would have been used to coming home late from work, doing homework, forgetting about dinner, and heading straight to bed for school in the morning. I have been doing this since I was 17 and my body is still not used to something like this.

"Since I'm not really in the mood to teach today I want you all to write a short poem and hand it in. Once you are done you are free to leave." Everyone in the class cheered and got to work.

I knew I wasn't going to leave out of here until it was time for class to end because I'm not as truly good at writing poems, but right now I have no choice but to come up with something.

I sat at my desk and thought for the last 10 minutes until something clicked in my mind and I let my pen do the writing for me.

In the deepest part of the mind, there is always something there that is pulling you to the dark side. Telling you that in that part of the mind everything is gold. Each day you lose yourself a little to that darkness, but you try to fight it, yet something is still making you want to reach out to the darkness.

You try your best to pull away, but the darkness shows you the truth about what is happening around you. What has happened to you and what will happen to the next person.

As you think about what the darkness is showing you, you start to think back to that one person that is at fault. The reason you are thinking about taking hold of the darkness and letting it control you.

You think about the pain that you were giving. You start thinking about the hurt you were feeling during that time. The more you think about it the darker your mind gets and the louder that voice gets you've been trying to push out.

Feeling hate, hurt, and pain you begin to scream to yourself and search for the person you blame for all this darkness. You think about the pain you want to cause them, the screams you want to hear from them.

Once your mind snapped back into reality you notice the blood and knife in your hand, and you looked down to see that the person you blame was yourself.

I was caught up in my writing that I didn't even notice that class had ended, and that Professor Smith was standing over my desk.

I looked up at her and saw the look of concern in her eyes. I wasn't for sure why she was looking at me like that until her finger lightly wiped the tears away that fell freely from my eyes.

"Is everything okay London?" This is the softest I heard her voice and it kind of scared me a little. I nodded my head and wiped the rest of my face and handed her my poem that I was for sure that wasn't a poem anymore.

"Sorry that I took too long with writing the poem, I didn't mean to overwrite," I tell her while I pack up my things getting ready for my next class.

"That's fine, I love reading your work. You write as if you are the character telling the story. As if you are living this yourself, it brings your writing to life." If only she knew that I was the character and that I am telling a story. I gave her a small smile and said goodbye and walked out of her classroom.

After my last class was over, I had to head home and get ready for work. Working in a restaurant doesn't pay much, but it does get the bills paid and last week I was given a raise.

I got home and took a quick shower and got dressed in my black dress pants, a white button-up shirt, with my black tie. I had to look around the room for my black work shoes since I just threw them somewhere in the room last night when I got home from work.

Once I found them, I looked at the time and notice I was running a little behind and needed to head out of the house if I wanted to make it on time in this New York traffic.

I got into my car and headed off to work. The only good thing about going to work is that I learn different things about people. Like what they like to eat and how they like their food. The sad part is I always see a lot of couples come in, making me wish that was me one day.

After 15 minutes of being in traffic, I finally pulled up to the restaurant and parked my car. I rushed out of the car and hurried into the restaurant, so I can clock in on time.

"Great you're here, I need you to take tables three, four, five, and six." My boss said behind me while I was clocking in. I nodded my head and grabbed my notepad and pen heading to table three.

"Hello, and welcome, I'm London and I'll be your waiter. What can I get you all to start off to drink?" I asked the three women that were sitting at table three.

"I'll take a sweet tea." The lady with pale white hair said.

"I'll take one as well." The lady with blonde hair spoke next.

"I'll just take a glass of water." The last woman said.

5

"Alright, I'll be right back with your drinks and to take your orders," I told them before walking away to fix their drinks.

I wonder why my boss got me doing more than three tables tonight. She never gives us more than that. I shrug my shoulders and make the drinks.

I took the drinks over to the table and took down their orders and handed it over to the cook.

The night was busy, but it went great. There were a lot of couples tonight, it was as if everyone had the same idea to take their loved ones out to dinner.

I was all over the restaurant, taking drink orders, taking orders, refilling drinks, and helping others with their tables.

This was one of the busiest nights that has ever been here, but I still love my job because I got it myself without any help from anyone else.

They say when you do something for yourself you love it more than you   will   when   someone   else   does   it   for   you.

Chapter 2

I have been walking around for years with this secret and now I have another secret to add to that. Sometimes secrets are good to keep, but most of the time they are not.

With both secrets running through my mind, I'm starting to think I am losing my mind slowly. I want to tell my best friend about this other secret that I have, but I'm not sure how she would react to it.

It's not that I'm scared of being judged, wait, that's exactly what I am afraid of. I'm scared of being judged; I'm scared of what someone else would think of me.

The only thing I am not scared of is Professor Smith reading my writing, I love when she reads it. It makes me feel a little bit of joy inside my body, that's why I can't wait to get back our essay and poem she had us write.

The week had come to an end, and the weekend was here. I don't go out over the weekend I try to pick up as many hours as I can at work to keep my best friend from asking me to go out with her.

I do go to the movies here and there, but I won't go to a club, it's too crowded and many different men try to pick up drunk girls in clubs. I try my best to stay away from things like that.

Yeah, it sounds crazy. I'm 23 and I don't go clubbing like other people my age, well it's just not for me and I don't like being touched.

There was a knock at my door, and I ran over from the couch to see who it was. Looking through the peephole I saw that it was Erica with food in her hands. I unlocked the door and open it up for her, helping her with the bags of food.

"I bring food, Chinese that you love oh so much." I grin with the feeling of excitement going through my body at the mention of food.

"You're the best, thanks for coming over," I said while grabbing an egg roll from her. It's nice how she knows me better than I know myself, a little weird but nice.

"I know you don't go out on the weekends and try to bury yourself in your work, but I wanted to know if we can have a girl's weekend here in your apartment?" I stared at her; she would give up her weekend just because I don't like going out.

"I would love that, Erica. It's been a while since we did something like that together, but I don't have any junk food in here." I told her while stuffing my face with food.

"That's fine I'll run out and grab some stuff."

"I'll come with you." She looked at me like I lost my head or something, I mean sure I don't like going out, but I do go to the stores when I need to.

We finish eating and then cleaned up our mess before heading out the door. I didn't want to drive, so we got into her car. I like driving sometimes but New York traffic will make you lose your mind.

No matter what time of day it is there is always traffic, but lucky for us we don't have to go that far to the store. Since it was the end of winter we didn't want to walk in the cold.

When we got into the store, we started grabbing all kinds of junk food that will last us until the weekend is over.

I went and grabbed ice cream while Erica went and got the cookies. We met back up in the candy aisle and grabbed different kinds of candy. When I looked in our basket, I notice Erica had grabbed chips and popcorn that I had forgotten all about.

The last thing we needed to grab was drinks and then check out.

Finally, we were back home and putting away most of the snacks and ice cream.

"What should we watch for the night?"

"Let's watch DC's: Legends of Tomorrow." I nodded my head and went on Netflix. I always wanted to watch this but never had the chance to.

Erica made some popcorn and brought us both a drink to the living room, while I grabbed the chips and candy.

"Thanks for doing this with me, I know you wanted to go out," I said while sitting down next to her.

"It's fine, I'll do anything to make you feel comfortable." I smiled at her and played the first episode in season 1.

I was watching the show, but I can feel Erica staring at me, I wasn't going to look at her because I didn't want to miss anything that was going to happen.

While still looking at the T.V. I used my hand and made her turn to look at it as well. I was starting to feel a little uncomfortable with her staring into my damn soul.

"How have you been doing lately? Still having them nightmares?" She asked me while pausing the show.

I took in a deep breath and finally looked at her. She is the only one I feel comfortable talking about this with.

"I'm always having nightmares. They're starting to get worst." I mumble.

"It will get better London; you're doing a lot better than you were when you were in high school. You never talked to anyone in school and look at you now talking with Professor Smith." I started feeling funny when she said our professor's name, and a smile came across my face.

"Oh, my lord, is London Wilson blushing?" She teased.

I shook my head so fast that I thought it was about to fall off. "I have no reason to blush," I said and started the show back up.

Spending time with my best friend like we used to, made me feel very happy and I can't remember the last time I truly felt happy.

I started thinking back to this secret I had been keeping from her. I wonder if this is a good time to tell her and see how she reacts.

I paused the T.V. and looked at her, "I want to tell you something, but I'm scared of how you will react."

"You can tell me anything, you know that London." I nodded my head and took a deep breath while getting my thoughts together.

"I-um, I think I'm gay," I whispered but loud enough for her to hear.

"What do you mean you think you're gay?" She asked me. Her tone was normal, but I was still nervous about this talk.

"Just that I believe I like girls."

"Do you have a crush on another girl or something?" I looked away and didn't answer her question.

I heard her gasp which made me turn around to look at her. "You do have a crush on someone, and I want to know who. This is amazing for you London." She yelled making me cover my ears.

"I can't tell you; I don't want you to think I'm weird."

"I can never think that about you."

I sat and talked with myself in my head, if anyone else would have seen this they would have thought I was crazy. I'm sure she can keep it a secret as well.

"It's Professor Smith," I mumble very low making her ask me again.

"Professor Smith," I whispered.

Her eyes look like they wanted to pop out of her head because of how wide they went. I had never seen my best friend speechless before, I thought that I had broken her for a minute until she started jumping up and down.

"Oh my gosh, London!" She screamed. I'm sure someone thinks she is getting killed or hurt in here by the way she keeps screaming and yelling.

"Would you lower your voice, are you trying to tell everyone in Mexico," I said and pulled her down from standing on my couch.

"I'm just very happy for you, I never thought I would hear you say you have a crush on someone and let alone a professor."

"You have to promise me you won't say anything to anyone or let it slip out your mouth." She nodded her head and held her pinkie up for me. I locked mine with hers and we shook on it.

I started the show back and we got back to watching the T.V. and stuffing our faces with junk food.

11

Not long after we were both getting sleepy but didn't want to stop the show because it was getting good, and we needed to see what was going to happen in the next episode.

Jumping out of my sleep from the feeling of someone shaking me, I wanted to scream and fight whoever the person was, but once my vision came back to me, I saw that it was only Erica.

She had concern written all over her face. I took my shirt and wiped the sweat that was on my forehead.

"You were screaming in your sleep for help."

I looked away from her and looked at the blank T.V. screen. I didn't like when she saw me like this, I already knew I was weak, but I didn't want her to know that I was weak as well.

She might be my best friend but there are still things I don't want her to know and being weak is one of those things.

"I try so hard to fight him off every time, but it always turns out the same."

I flinch when I felt her hand touch me, but I settled down a little after. She laid behind me on the couch and held me close to her like she always did when she stayed the night.

She was the only person that I would let touch me, and well now Professor Smith. I didn't flinch when Professor Smith touched my face to remove away the tears that were falling down my cheek.

"It's going to be okay Lolo; everything will be fine." She whispered in my ear while rubbing her hand up and down my back.

I let out a sigh and closed my eyes hoping that sleep comes soon and that the dreams don't come back.

Chapter 3

Waking up on a Monday morning after the weekend I had with Erica was a bit hard, but I pushed myself through the laziness.

That was the first time I was lazy and did not think about work. It was a nice thing because I feel more relaxed and not as stressed out. I need to start doing more weekends like that and slowly build myself back up again.

Finally, I pulled myself out of bed and headed into the bathroom to do my morning routine. Showering, brushing, and doing my make-up.

Once I was done with everything I walked into my closet and looked for something to wear. I looked at the dress Erica made me buy a few months ago when she begged me to go shopping with her.

I pulled out the dress that was blood red with long sleeves and hung off the shoulder a little. I looked through my shoes and grabbed some black heels.

I know I'm only going to school, but this is the first time I truly felt comfortable in my skin. Not only that I might be taking on Erica's advice and dressing to impress. I want to get Professor Smith's attention.

Even though Erica said she thinks the Professor has a thing for me, I don't believe it.

I got dressed and straighten my hair after I looked in the mirror, I was happy with my look. I checked the time and saw I had 45 minutes left to get to school and class.

I grabbed my bag and keys and head to my car. I get into the car and start it up pulling out of the apartment parking lot.

I head to school in this New York traffic. Lucky for me that this traffic wasn't as bad, and I made it to school with 15 minutes to spare.

I walked to the Café part of the school and saw Erica sitting there with two coffees, gosh I hope one of them is for me.

"Please tell me one of them is for me! I don't have time to stand in line for a coffee."

"Of course, one is for you. I notice that you weren't here early and went and grabbed one for you." I thanked her and took the coffee.

"Damn, you trying to pull the Professor huh?" I hurried and covered her mouth and looked around making sure no one heard her.

"Would you keep it down?! Are you trying to tell the whole damn school?!" I whispered yelling.

She shook her head, and I removed my hand from over her mouth. I grabbed her hand and pulled her out of the Café and headed toward our English class.

"But I don't think you should be a shame of who you like. You know that Brianna girl?"

15

I had to think for a while before nodding my head. "She is dating Professor William, and everyone knows about them. Hell, a lot of Professors are dating their students."

I stopped and stared at her like she had two heads or something. "Wait, you're telling me that all these Professors are dating their students and the school knows about it?"

"Yeah, they just need to be harder on them during class, so no one thinks they are passing because of who they're dating."

Well, it wouldn't matter if Professor Smith is harder on me because I am already passing her class and I know almost everything she is teaching, and what I don't know I learn fast.

We started back walking and heading to class.

Once we made it to the door of our class I stop and looked over at Erica, "do I look okay?"

She nodded her head and gave me a big smile while pulling me into the classroom. When we walked in, a few students were sitting at their desks and their heads turned toward us.

"Good morning," I said before taking my seat.

I didn't hear anything back from them, so I looked up to see them still staring. Okay, this is getting uncomfortable.

I leaned over and whispered into Erica's ear, "why are they staring like that?"

"Because everyone is so used to your jeans and t-shirts, plus you look sexy as hell." She said while laughing.

I shrugged my shoulders and pulled out my notebook. Not long after more people came in and some stared as well.

Soon later Professor Smith walked in as well. "Good morning class, I hope you all had an amazing weekend."

Some cheered and some groaned, I guess they partied too hard and forgot they had a class on Monday. That's why I don't go out, I don't need to be waking up with a hangover.

After she put her things down at her desk she turned and looked around the class, and once her eyes got to me, they almost popped out of her head.

Okay, I'm starting to think this was a bad idea. I looked away from her and started drawing in my notebook.

I'm not sure if it's a good thing that people keep staring at me or if it's a bad thing. A few people told me I look different but good different. That left me a little confused, but I shrugged it off.

Soon Professor Smith started talking, "Okay, I went over your essays and poems from last week. Most of them were amazing and some needed a little work. You will know what you need to work on once you read my comment."

She started passing back the essays and poems. I was the last one to get back my essay and poem.

"Your essay was amazing London like always, and your poem seems so real. I just wanted to read it over again." I gave her a small smile and thanked her.

If only she knew that it was real, and I have been fighting the dark part of my mind, and I am slowly losing myself to the darkness.

She had us read three chapters in the book that we got at the beginning of the semester. We had to write a 2page essay on the three chapters.

I was glad that we got to do the essay at home and all we had to do in class was read the book, something about her wanting to make sure that we read the book and not just look up things to write about.

"London may you stay after class please?" I heard Professor Smith ask. I nodded my head and watch the rest of the students get their things together and leave out the class.

Once everyone was gone, she walked over to the door and closed it before coming over and sitting next to me.

"I wanted to ask you about your writing. You don't have to answer if you don't want to." I nodded and waited for her to continue.

"Your writing always feels real when I'm reading it, and I wanted to know if it was real?"

I looked down at my hands and played with my fingers, I want to tell her that it was real and that I did live through that. Writing about what has happened in my life is the only way for me to get it out.

"I- um no, it's not real." *Lie.*

I lied right to her, and I can see that she knew I lied to her, but I'm not ready to talk about this with anyone else. I need to think about this first.

I do feel comfortable with her around me when she touches me it feels like everything went away. The pain, the hurt, the nightmares, they all seem to just vanish away from me, and I never want her touch to leave my body.

I didn't notice I was staring until her face started turning red. I giggled a little and her head snapped back up to me.

"I never heard you giggle or laugh before, and it's the most beautiful sound I have ever heard." I guess she heard what she just said because her eyes popped wide open, and my face was starting to heat up.

"Um let me walk you to Professor William's class." I nodded my head and grabbed my things and walked out of the classroom with her.

While walking to my next class it was nothing but silence between us, it wasn't awkward it was just silence.

"Thank you." She looked confused when I said that. "Thanks for the compliment, no one has ever said something nice like that to me before, but Erica and that's only because she is my best friend."

"Well, it's nothing to thank me over."

"Of course, there is. You didn't have to, but you did."

19

She smiled, and I smiled at her back and the silence begins again.

We got to Professor William's class and just stood there for a minute. "I hope the rest of your day goes wonderful and you look very beautiful by the way." She said before opening the door for me.

"She was with me, William." He nodded his head and told me to take my seat, which was next to Erica.

She leaned over and whispered to me, "what did she want to talk about with you?"

"She wanted to know was my poem real, I told her that they weren't, but I don't think she believes me. Good thing she didn't push me to tell her." I whispered back.

I can still feel my face heating up from her calling me beautiful. It also made me happy that she noticed I looked different today.

One of these days I am going to get the courage and ask her on a date but before I can do that, I need to get myself together and fight off my demons.

Chapter 4

Leaving my apartment for work I felt like I was being watched. I looked over my shoulders and didn't see anyone, I shrugged it off and got into the car.

I pulled off from the apartments and headed toward work with that same feeling following me. Maybe I'm just being paranoid because of the dream I had last night.

I made it into work 10 minutes early, I clocked in and went to talk with my boss about getting tomorrow off.

I knocked on the office door and heard a come in, I opened the door and walked in. "Hey boss, I wanted to know if I can get tomorrow off, I have a doctor's appointment and don't want to miss it." I lied.

Well, I didn't lie, I'm going to go talk with someone like Erica asked me to do. She wants me to get help and thinks that's what I need to move on from this.

"Sure, I'll just double your weekend next week." I nodded my head and left out the office grabbing my notepad and heading to my assigned tables.

I couldn't shake the feeling that I was still being watched, but I didn't let it get to me since I am in a place I love.

21

I smiled at the customers and took down all the drink orders for the tables I was waiting for. I don't want to have to come back and forth taking drink orders.

I grabbed the drinks for the three tables and took them over to them and took down their orders.

I wanted to make my job a lot easier, and I wanted to get this night over with, so I can go back home where I feel safe.

The night dragged on and seemed like it would never come to an end, but when it finally did, I clocked out and headed to my car to go home.

I drove around a little bit just to make sure I wasn't being followed, I don't care if I'm being paranoid or whatever, I'm making sure I am safe.

I finally pulled up to the apartments and turned the car off, before getting out I looked out the window and looked around the parking lot. Everything seems to be normal as always.

I got out of the car and walked up to my apartment getting ready to unlock the door.

"Unlock the door and don't make a sound or you will regret it." Came a deep voice, a voice I know all too well.

With my hand shaking, I tried my best to hurry and unlock the door. When the door was open, I was pushed inside, and I heard the door being locked.

"I have been looking all over for you baby girl. You been gone for 6 years and didn't even show up to speak with your mother and me." His deep voice raised.

"I-I don't want anything to do with you and the woman that gave birth to me." Once I said that I felt a hard slap come across my face.

"Don't talk about your mother like that!" His yell made me jump and whimper.

I held my face and looked up at him, "what do you want from me?"

"There is no need to tell you when I can just show you." He walked over to me, and I started walking backward trying to get away from him. Throughout these 6 years, I thought I have finally become safe, but I guess that was a lie.

He pushed me up against the wall hard and I whimper from the pain that went through my back.

"You left me with your mother who can't give it to me as you can." His voice getting raspy. I didn't say anything and just looked at him.

Feeling his hand rub up against my side made me flinch and made him angry.

Without another thought, he snatches my shirt open and pulled it off me, not long after my bra was on the floor with my shirt.

I felt the tears running down my face with every move his hand made. Not long after his mouth was on my breast sucking hard until the nipple was as hard as a diamond.

"Please stop!" I knew all too well that's what he wanted to hear, for me to beg for him to stop. I didn't want him to touch me like this.

He slapped me across the face, and I fell to the floor holding my face and crying. He got on top of me and started back sucking on my breast.

I started fighting him back, this needed to stop, and it needs to stop now but he was stronger than me. He held my hands above my head and went back to what he was doing.

"Mm yours is so much better than your mother's, I missed them for the last 6 years." His hot breath fanned my skin.

Soon I felt him trying to get my pants off and I started fighting back harder which caused me to get a punch to the face.

I lay there and allowed him to do whatever he wanted to me. I felt my pants coming off and my legs being pulled apart.

Laying here with every image of him on top of me coming into my mind and with this one being added to it.

I screamed out when I felt him entering me, that same hurtful pain growing through my body and the same tears that fell each time he did this.

He was supposed to protect me, keep me safe, and run boys away. Make me feel like his princess. Which he did until I turned 13 and things started to change. I started to look older, and he started to drink more.

Mother was just there not caring about what happened, if she had her drugs, she didn't care what he did.

I had no one there to protect me, my grandparents had died when I was 9 and 10. They were the only ones who truly loved me in this family.

My mother and father were the only children, so I didn't have any uncles or aunts.

"Damn your just as tight as I remember when you were younger." He moaned out.

With each pump he made, more tears fell.

"Shit I'm coming fast. Lucky for you, you get to feel my sperm for the first time." Before I can understand what was said, I felt something hot go inside me and my eyes popped open.

No, no, no, no this can't be. He wasn't satisfied with raping me that he had to put his sperm inside me.

"Now I can finally see you birth my child." He moaned out.

I turned my head toward the wall that he had pushed me up against and noticed the table I put there when I first moved in here.

I remember when I had placed a lot of different knives around the house because I was scared, he would find me, but I didn't think about that at the time of being scared.

I glance out the corner of my eye and saw he still had his eyes closed. I slowly reach for the knife that was under the table, but I didn't move slow enough because he noticed that I was moving and started beating me.

Taking each of his punches I still tried to reach for the knife, once I had it in my hand, I stabbed him in the chest hoping that I hit something that will make him bleed out.

His face had a shocked look on it before he fell on top of me. I pushed him off and crawled over to the wall and hugged my knees to my chest. I put my face on my knees and cried.

I can't believe I just did that; I just threw my whole life away.

I jumped when I heard a loud knock at the door.

"Open up, it's the police." I heard. I started to panic and didn't move from my spot. The knocking started again and yet I still didn't move from my seat.

Then the door burst open, and people started running inside. Policemen and women everywhere.

"Drop the knife ma'am." A policewoman said to me. I dropped the knife and stayed where I was.

No clothes on, blood on me, and tears running down my face.

"I didn't mean to do it, I just wanted him to stop."

"I couldn't take it no more. So many years of rape and beatings." I said to no one.

The policewoman pulled off her jacket and put it around my shoulders. I had no one here with me, I needed someone to hold on to and she was the only one next to me.

I hugged her and cried more.

"It's going to be okay, your safe. You did nothing wrong." She whispered while letting me hug her.

I didn't know what was going on around me, so I looked to where the policemen and women were and saw they were over my father's body.

The officer that let me hug her pulled my head away. "You don't have to look at that."

She lifted me and started walking toward the door while they were putting him in a body bag.

"Is there anyone we could call for you?" I nodded my head and pointed to my bag where my phone was. She told another officer to grab the bag and get the phone out.

I was shaking too badly and couldn't get to the number I wanted to call.

I told her the name in my phone to call and my name.

"Hello Erica, this is officer Jones we are here with London.

Chapter 5

I lay in the hospital bed while they did a rape kit on me. I already know what they're going to find, but they want to make sure I killed him in self-defense.

Honestly, even if I went to jail for killing him I would do it all over again, he needed to stop by going to jail or being killed.

The other worst thing about this is that I had to tell them about all the other times he had been raping me and how my mother just sat there and let him.

I heard something going on outside in the hallway and not long after Erica came running in with a nurse following behind her.

"Ma'am you-"

"Listen, lady, whenever it comes down to her no one will keep me from making sure she is okay, now shut the hell up and let me be." Erica cut her off.

"It's okay, she is the one the officer had called." The nurse nodded her head and left-back out of the room.

"Oh gosh, Lolo! I can't believe he did this again." She hugged me and brushed her face against mine making me wince in pain.

She pulled away and looked at my face seeing the bruised there and tears begin to fall from her eyes.

"Don't cry, I'm okay now," I said while wiping her face.

That's how close I and her are when one is hurt the other one will cry with the other one.

"Okay, I got everything I need. I will get you some pain medicine and you will be free to leave. I'm sorry this has happened to you, and you did what anyone else would in this situation." The doctor spoke.

"I already know what the test will show, but they need it for their records." I nodded my head at her and snuggled closer to Erica.

The doctor left the room leaving me and Erica alone.

"Can you tell me what happened?"

"Like any other weekend I was on my way to work but this time I just had a feeling I was being followed. I shrugged it off and went to work."

"A-and when I got to work, I still had that same feeling and it was starting to scare me, I thought I was losing my mind and just being paranoid. I got off work and went home and before getting out of the car I looked around to make sure everything was normal like always. When I got to the door, he was there behind me." I cried out.

She started rocking me back and forth while crying herself. "Everything is going to be okay Lolo. Your safe now he is long gone."

"Erica, where am I going to live now? I can never go back to that apartment."

"You're coming to stay with me, I got a 2 bedroom for a reason and some of your clothes are already there from when you spent the night." I nodded my head and held on to her tighter.

Erica is only a year older than me, and I see her as my big sister. She is the only one that has ever been there for me, without her I don't know what I would have done.

The nurse came in with some pain pills which I am very thankful for because my face and ribs are killing me.

Nothing was broken but there was a lot of bruising and they had to take a lot of pictures.

When the nurse left, officer Jones walked in. "You were very brave London, and I'm proud that you stopped a monster while you had the chance to."

"I have a little girl at home waiting for me to get off work and I don't know what I would have done if that was her, but your mother didn't give a damn what happens to you, and I can't wait to lock her up." She growled scaring me a little.

"Sorry for that, I just hate when parents don't protect their kids from monsters like him. I'll keep in touch with you and see how you are doing, I have a friend and told her about your case, but I didn't tell her anything. She said she will see you whenever you're ready." I nodded my head and took the two cards she was passing to me.

31

One is her number, and the other is her friend's work number. Erica took the cards from me and put them in her purse.

"Thanks for calling me, Officer Jones." They shook hands. "No problem, she needed someone there that she could trust. Make sure she goes and talks with that person." She said while pointing at Erica's purse.

She left out the room and Erica turned and looked at me. "Are you going to go?"

I nodded my head to her answer. I needed to go, I needed to see someone, I needed to get better for myself but there was one thing I wanted to do before I went and talk with that doctor.

"I'm not going to school for a while, can you let our professor know that I have been in an accident?"

"Of course, and don't worry I will make sure to get your work for you." I smiled at her because she knew what I was about to say next.

Just because he did this to me doesn't mean I will let it get me off track. I needed to finish school, I wanted to finish school, I wanted to be something that my parents weren't. I wanted to do something they thought was a waste of time.

They never even finish high school, and I was not going to end up like them.

"Okay Ms. Wilson you are free to go, the results will be in about a week or two. I will call you when they are in, and officer Jones asked me to call her as well when they come in.

"Okay, thank you for your help."

"That's what I'm here for, stay safe, and don't let this break you down."

"Um I came here in just Officer Jones's jacket; I don't have any clothes here."

She nodded her head and walked out and came back a few minutes later with some sweatpants and a t-shirt. I gave a quick thank you before she left back out the door.

The pain medicine they gave me was starting to kick in and I was feeling great. I felt like I was going in slow motion putting on the shirt.

Erica took the shirt out of my hands and helped me put it on along with the sweatpants. I didn't even have any shoes with me, but I didn't care about that.

"Come on, let's get you home and into bed." I smiled and allowed her to help me off the bed.

Thanks to the medicine I don't feel the pain in my ribs as much but trust me it's there.

While leaving the hospital I thank everyone for helping me, the nurse who gave me the medicine started laughing saying that the medicine got me feeling good right now.

They told us we can pick up any painkillers over the counter.

I woke up from being shaken and looked over to Erica, "come on we're here."

I got out of the car and waited for her to lock up the car and come beside me. Not because I was scared but because I needed someone to lean on.

I'm too sleepy to walk on my own and I don't want to fall and have her trying to help me back up. I'm glad we don't have to go up any stairs.

She unlocked the door and I walked in heading straight to her room. I know it's another room in here but, I don't want to be alone tonight.

"Let's get you to the shower before you go to bed." I heard Erica say before going into the bathroom.

Okay, I'm starting to think she is enjoying treating me like a baby. I mean I do love the attention, but she doesn't need to run my shower for me.

Since we were comfortable with each other I started taking my clothes off and heading toward the shower, so I can get this over with and go to bed.

I took a quick shower and got dressed in the nightclothes she put out for me.

I lay in the bed and waited for her to finish her shower.

If you were someone that was on the outside of our friendship you would think we were a couple, but we're not. She is my sister and my best friend.

She finally came out and got into bed, and I snuggled closer to her.

"Thanks for being there for me," I whispered.

"There is nothing to thank me for, I'll always be there for you. You're my baby sister and I need to protect you." She whispered back.

"I love you, Erica."

"I love you too Lolo."

I smiled after hearing her say it back to me, I closed my eyes and let sleep take me over again.

Chapter 6

It's only been a few days since everything happened and I still haven't been back to school. Erica brings me my homework and the classwork, lucky for me it's everything that we already went over.

I had to do some math work, an essay, and 2 poems. I'm glad these were the only 2 classes I had because I didn't want to be doing all this work.

Right now, I am laying across the bed looking at something on Netflix and eating a bowl of ice cream.

I haven't been able to go outside because every time I do I start to panic and run back into the house. I know he can't hurt me anymore but that doesn't stop the fear that runs through my body.

Within these few days, I have been talking more to officer Jones and it's been making me feel a little better.

Today she made me promise that I would go talk to her therapist friend, which brings me to the thought that I should be getting ready because Erica will be home soon to take me.

I got up and went into the bathroom. I ran the shower and got undressed and hopped in. I let the water run over my body before I start to wash my body and hair.

I got out and dried myself off and blow-dried my hair. I wrapped the towel around me and went and grabbed my underwear. I grabbed some black skinny jeans and a white t-shirt.

I didn't care about what I wear to see this lady because I didn't want to go but I don't like breaking promises.

After I finished getting ready Erica walked through the door yelling that I better be ready.

"I'm ready don't get your granny panties in a twist." I joked and ran from her before she can hit me.

"Okay, come on before you be late." I sigh and follow her out the door.

We got into the car, and I gave her the address to where this place was at. I was hoping that it be so much traffic that she would want to turn around, but I guess I wasn't lucky enough because we got there in 10 minutes.

I stayed in my seat with my seat belt on and looked out the window at the building I'm supposed to be going in.

"Are you coming in with me?" I questioned. She nodded her head and turned the car off.

"I wouldn't let you go through this by yourself, but I would make you go through this because it's what you need. It's time for you to be happy and not have to fear the outdoors."

I took my seat belt off and got out of the car with her. I can feel the nerves in me going crazy inside and begging for me to get back into the car and get the hell out of here.

I closed my eyes and took in some deep breaths. I felt Erica's hand grab mine giving me the reassurance I needed and letting me know that she is here every step of the way.

I gave a weak smile and started walking with her by my side.

Having a best friend like Erica is amazing, I'm glad I have her by my side because I don't know what I'll do if I didn't have her.

We walked into the building and up to the front desk.

"I have an appointment today with Dr. Morris," I told the lady sitting at the desk.

"What's your name?"

"London Wilson."

She started typing something on the computer and a few minutes later she had me sitting down in a chair next to Dr. Morris's office.

She said that she was just finishing up with another client and would be ready for me in a few minutes.

I took this time to look around the area, there were all kinds of photos hanging on the wall. All of them with the same one person in them, that must be the doctor and the rest must be the clients she helped get better.

I wonder would I be one of those clients or would not be fixable.

"London Wilson, you can come in now." I heard someone say.

I looked up to the door to the room that was opened, and Dr. Morris was standing there with a big smile on her face.

I looked over to Erica and she nodded her head smiling at me, I smiled back and got up following the doctor back into the room.

"You can have a seat on the chair or lay down on the couch whichever you feel comfortable with." I nodded my head and sat in the chair.

I looked around her office and it was giving off a warm welcoming feeling and I was liking that. I didn't want to feel uncomfortable, but I know I already do.

"I'm Dr. Morris as you already know and I'm just here to listen, whatever you say in this room I will not speak outside of this room unless I believe you are a threat to yourself and others."

Well, that's a good thing but I already know she might tell whatever we talk about to officer Jones but that's fine with me.

"Officer Jones told me about you and some of your story. I didn't let her tell me much because that is for you to do when you are ready." I listened to her and didn't speak.

"First things first, why are you here?"

I sat and thought about it for a while. Why am I here? Is it because I made a promise? Or was it because I know I needed help.

"I'm not sure, I made a promise that I will come, and I don't like breaking promises."

"Do you believe you need help?"

I slowly nodded my head and looked back at the door then turned around to look back at her.

She was writing something down on her notepad and looked back up at me.

"It's good that you know that you need help, now tell me your story."

I sat here and just stared at her, I wasn't ready to just come out and tell my story to this stranger. I didn't know her, and I didn't want her to know everything about my terrible life.

I went from staring at her to looking back at the door and back to her. I did that back and forth until I finally gave up and started telling her my story.

"Growing up from a baby until I was 12 was an amazing life. My parents didn't have it all, but they still made a way to give me a good life, I thought my parents couldn't do no wrong and that they were the best parents anyone can ask for."

Once I started talking about my story it was like everything just poured out of me and didn't want to stop.

"Every birthday I had we would go to the park and spend all day there having a picnic there. Mom would bring the cake and dad would forget to grab the ice cream and would go back home just to get it. Each birthday that passed was the best one after the next until I turned 13." I felt something run down my cheek.

"M-my 13th birthday started the same and everything seems to be just how it always was but mother looked sick this time, and father was happier than usual. That night I did everything I always did. Take a shower, say goodnight to my parents and go to bed for school. In the middle of that, I heard my mom and father fighting, but I didn't know about what. Soon after my dad came into my room and sat down on my bed and kissed me on the forehead like always." I paused taking in some deep breaths.

"He hugged me close and whispered in my ear *'Daddy is not happy with mommy right now do you want to make daddy happy again?'* Of course, me being his daughter I wanted him to be happy, so I nodded my head and asked what I can do to make him happy again?" I laugh and grab one of the tissues from the table.

"He grabbed my hand and place it in the middle of his pants and said just rub and do as daddy say. I went to take my hand away, but he stopped me and said this is what's going to make daddy happy. I was only a kid and didn't want to make him unhappy more than what he was already, I started doing what he said and the next thing he started taking off his clothes and getting into bed with me."

I looked off into space as the memories came rushing back to me from that first night all this began. The fear I felt, the love I felt for him left my heart without a trace.

"London are you still with me?"

Her voice snapped me out of the memory, "Yes."

"You don't have to finish if you don't want to."

"No, I-I need to finish, I need this off my mind and chest."

"Okay, whenever you're ready." I nodded my head and took in a deep breath.

"The night he got into bed with me he whispered, *'I'm going to show you how mommy and daddy love each other,'* each move he made another piece of my clothes was taken off. I felt him touch my lady part and I tried to move because I was 13 and I knew no one was supposed to touch you there. He slapped me and told me to stay still, and I did as I was told." I wiped the tears that were still falling.

"I never knew someone can feel so much pain like that, it hurt so bad. I kept saying daddy it hurts please stop, p-please it hurt. His words were *'Just a second baby girl daddy's about to show you.'* At that time, I didn't know what he was about to show me until I felt something on my tummy."

"That went on for 4 years, the sad part about it was mother didn't even care. I told her a few nights after it happened because she wasn't anywhere to be found when it first happened, and she said just to make daddy happy, so mommy can be happy too and she went and took out a needle and stuck herself. I asked what she was taken she said it was her medicine." I giggled, medicine yea right.

"During those times I didn't have no one until I met Erica in high school. It was something about her that made me trust her, that made me want to tell her what's been going on in my household. I guess I made the right choice because she's still by my side through everything I went through. Her family is the reason I was able to leave my parents at the age of 17."

"What do you mean they're the reason you were able to leave?"

"When I would go over every time, they would notice that I didn't like to be touched but would only let Erica touch me. They started seeing the bruises and started asking what was happening to me. I couldn't tell them the truth, so I just said that I need to get away from my parents because of the beatings. I told them part of the truth and they wanted to help me get a job and a place to live, but I just asked them that when I find a job, can they take me to my interview. We agreed on that and everything felt like it was coming together."

I looked back at the door again, it's starting to become a habit of mine and I don't know why.

"You keep staring at the door is something wrong?"

"It's a habit I just picked up since everything that happened. I have to keep watching my back, even though I know he is gone."

"Want to finish telling me how you are feeling?"

43

I told her yes and got back to telling her everything. "The night I killed him was the first time he saw me in 6 years. I thought I was safe for good, but I guess I was wrong. That night he told me that I was old enough to give him a child and he came inside me."

Her eyes popped open; you can see the surprised look on her face. The crazy thing is I didn't tell anyone that part but her and I don't know why.

"Have you told Officer Jones?" I shook my head no.

"Have you told the doctors at the hospital?"

"No, they wanted to do a pregnancy test on me, but I didn't let them. I didn't want to know if there will be a chance, I'll be having his child, but I'm sure they will find something on the rape kit that was done."

She looked at her watch and back up at me. "Seem like we have come to an end for your hour, but I'm very proud of you. Most people would just sit here and stare at me and not say a thing, but you want help and you opened up to get that help."

I gave her a weak smile and she smiled back at me, "It's nice to see you smile, keep working on getting the help that smile of yours would never leave your face. I don't usually tell my clients this but take up some kickboxing and you would truly feel safe because you would know how to protect yourself."

We said our goodbyes and I made another appointment to see her again. After talking with her it felt nice to not walk around with this by myself anymore and someone wanted to help me get through it.

I walked out of her office and saw that Erica was sitting there on her phone. I walked up to her and tapped her on the shoulder making her jump.

She stood up and pulled me into a hug, I guess she saw the dried tears on my face.

"Are you okay?" I nodded my head and hugged her back tight.

"I'm fine now and there is something I need to tell you but I'm not sure when I'll be ready to tell you, so give me some time and you will find out."

Chapter 7

It's been over two weeks since the last time I spoke with Dr. Morris, but she has been having Officer Jones call and check up on me making sure I'm okay.

I still haven't been back to school yet, but Erica told me our professors told me to take all the time I need, and that Professor Smith is truly worried about me.

I smiled at the thought that she is worried about me, maybe when it's her office hours I'll stop by and give her a visit I'm just not ready to be around so many people at once.

Since it's been two weeks the test from the rape kit is in and they want me down at the police station. Erica is coming with me and I'm happy about that, I didn't want to have to go through this alone.

"Thanks for coming with me."

"There is no need to thank me, you're my sister and I'll stand beside you no matter what."

That alone made me smile. I turned back toward the window and watch the buildings pass by us as she drove toward the station.

Not long after we were pulling up and she was parking the car. I looked at the building and watch different officers come and go.

I looked over at her and gave her a smile before getting out of the car. I walked into the building and asked for Officer Jones. Since that is the only Officer, I know.

We waited for a good 10 minutes before she came out and told us to follow her.

We walked into her office, and I notice a picture on her desk of a little girl. I picked it up and smiled at it.

"That's Lizzy, my daughter." I heard her say over my shoulders making me jump.

"She's beautiful," I mumble.

We took a seat in front of her desk and waited for another 5 minutes until someone walked into the room.

"London this is my boss, Agent Danvers."

I shook her hand, "Nice to meet you."

I nodded and looked back at Jones. "I don't get why I'm here?"

"You're here because I wanted to let you know that the case is closed, well there wasn't a case because you did what you had to do to protect yourself." I heard Agent Danvers say.

47

"We have your mother in custody if you want to speak with her."

I froze when I heard what Jones said. I haven't seen her in 6 years, or you can say I truly haven't seen her since I was 14 because she was always out getting high and leaving me alone with a rapist.

I took in a deep breath and tried to pull the tears back in. The last time I spoke with Dr. Morris, she told me that the only way I will truly get past this is if I talked with my mother.

I nodded my head, "yes I'll like to speak with her."

I got up and followed Agent Danvers out of the room and down the hall where they keep their prisoner before they are sent somewhere else.

The closer we got to the cells the more I was starting to regret doing this, but I knew it was what I needed, and I wasn't going to let fear scare me this time.

I looked at each cell we pass with someone in it thinking that it was her, but when we finally stopped in front of a cell the person that was in it didn't look like my mother. They looked sick and too skinny for the woman I remember as my mother.

"Wilson someone is here to see you." Agent Danvers yelled loud enough to make her look up.

"I'll be down the hall when you're ready to go back." I nodded my head and watched her walk away.

"It's been what, 6 years since the last time I have seen you kid?"

48

I chuckle at the fact she just called me a kid and then anger started to replace that chuckle and I just wanted to slap her.

"I'm not a kid anymore mother! I'm not that little girl you let get raped!" I screamed.

"What do you want then?"

"I just wanted to know why? Why didn't you protect me? Why didn't you keep him away from me? Why did you have to go to drugs?" I sent question after question to her not giving her a chance to answer them.

"Drugs was all I knew after you turned 13. He asked me if he can have you that night, I told him no, that you were our daughter, and we fought that night. It was the first time he hit me; I didn't go into your room to check on you, I just left the house. I met someone that night who said they can make me feel better and gave me some drugs and honestly it did make me feel better."

I looked at her and I couldn't believe what she was saying. She didn't come to check on me, she didn't call the police, she just left.

"After that night on drugs that's all I wanted and cared about. Your father even started doing it and since he was giving me what I want, I gave him you in return." She said with no emotions.

She didn't even care that she gave up her only child to a rapist, she didn't care that I started cutting myself. She just didn't give a fuck about anything but her and her drugs.

49

I left from in front of the cell and walked down the hall where Agent Danvers went to. Before I got too far, she spoke again.

"It's crazy, I keep calling him your father because I know he isn't your father and I think he knew that as well. That's why he wanted you so bad because he knew I cheated on him and he didn't care about you anymore after finding out the truth."

I started back walking toward the area Agent Danvers was at.

I found her at someone's desk and told her I wanted to go back to where Jones and Erica were at. I needed to get out of here, I needed to get some fresh air.

After all these years she could have done something to stop all this, she could have protected me, but she gave me to him because she knew I wasn't his child.

We walked back into the office, and I ran into Erica's arms and hugged her tight. This was all I truly need. My sister.

"Shh...Everything's going to be okay, I got you Lolo." She whispered in my ear.

Her words made me cry harder because that's true, she always had me, and I had her as well.

I pulled away and wiped my face and looked at Officer Jones.

"Thanks for all your help."

"I'm just doing my job, so there is no need to thank me." She said with a smile.

I went to return the smile, but I ran over to the trash can and started throwing up. I haven't eaten anything bad, so I don't know why this is happening.

I felt someone rubbing my back, but I couldn't look up because I was still throwing up. It's like it didn't want to stop.

When it finally did, Agent Danvers gave me some wipes and some crackers.

"That should help with the upset stomach." She said as I took them.

This is not the first time I threw up but I'm starting to think that I am getting sick.

"How long has this been going on?" Jones asked.

"A few days," Erica answered before me.

I looked at her because I didn't know she was paying that much attention to me.

"We should get you to a doctor." They all said at the same time.

I shook my head no because I already know what is wrong with me. I took a test before Erica got home from school. I was lucky that she kept some in her bathroom, for what reason I don't know.

51

"I already know what's wrong," I spoke as I went inside my purse pulling out the test.

I gave it to Erica and looked away at something else other than them. I didn't want their pity. I heard them gasp but I still didn't look at them.

"Why didn't you tell me?" I heard Erica say.

"I was going to tell you when you got back from school, but Officer Jones called, and we left right away," I told her honestly.

"What are you going to do?" Agent Danvers asked.

"I'm not sure yet, but I believe I might keep it."

"Are you sure about that?" Jones asked me.

I nodded my head with a smile. I could never give this child up no matter how they got here. They didn't ask to be here, and I wasn't going to take my anger out on them because they had no part of this.

"I'm sure before I got here, I was thinking about this on the way here. Like how I'm going to raise a child who had the same father as me, and how was I going to tell my child that we have the same father but now I don't have to tell them that because the guy I thought was my father was never my father."

They all looked surprised by what I said and honestly, I'm still a little surprised myself, but I'm also happy that my child and I wouldn't have the same father.

It's only one thing that's bothering me though, what would I say to them when they asked about their father? Do I just tell them the truth, or do I lie to them?

I started breathing harder and sweat started to show up on my forehead. I think I am having a panic attack. What if they start to hate themselves after finding out how they got here? Oh god, do I tell them that I killed their father while he was on top of me?

Okay, London, calm down. Your baby is not here yet everything is fine for now, don't worry about any of that right now. I kept telling myself over again.

"Lolo follow my breathing." I put all my attention on Erica and did as she did, and my breathing started to even out.

"Now what just happen? Why did you panic?" She asked me.

"I started thinking about the what-ifs and the next thing I know I started to panic. Erica what would I tell him/her?" I asked her with tears in my eyes.

She pulled me into her and hugged me tight, "I don't know sweetie, but we will get through this together, you're not alone I'm here for you."

Chapter 8

After we left the police station Erica talked me into going to see Dr. Morris because she was worried about me having another panic attack and because I didn't tell her what I was thinking about when it happened.

I'll tell her anything she wanted to know but I just didn't want to tell her right away. I wanted to make myself okay with how I thought things will turn out.

I called Dr. Morris and asked her if I can do a walk-in today and she said she was free for the next few hours. Now Erica is taking me straight there.

I'm sure we were at least 30 minutes away from Dr. Morris's office, but Erica got us there in 10 minutes.

She parked the car and we both got out and went inside the building and straight to Dr. Morris's office.

I guess she told her assistant that I was coming because I was told to go right in.

I knocked on the door and opened it after hearing a come-in.

I greeted her with a warm smile, and she gave me one back in return.

"Good evening, London."

"Good evening, Dr. Morris," I said while taking a seat on the couch.

"What brings you here today?"

"More like who?" I mumble.

She gave me a confused look and I started telling her what happened today at the station. Of course, she is glad that Erica made me come in today.

"Well, what started your panic?" She questioned.

"After I told them that my baby and I won't have the same father I started thinking about what if's." She nodded her head letting me know that she is listening.

"Like what if he/she asked about him? Or what if they want to know how they were born? Like do I tell them the truth, or do I lie to them? What if they start hating themselves because of who their father is? I was just thinking about all these things and the next thing I know I started breathing heavy and my chest felt like it was getting tight."

She started writing on her notepad and then looked back up at me. "I never had a client like this, but what I will tell you is to not worry about that now. Don't even worry about it when they come, when they get old enough and ask about it then you think about what to tell them and I say go with the truth. After you do tell them, let them know it's not their fault."

I smiled at her and wiped the tears I didn't know I had come down. Each time I talk to her she always knows what to say. Now I can tell Erica the truth.

We finish up the session and said our goodbyes, she told me to come when I feel the need to. I left out her office and walked up to Erica and hugged her while thanking her for making me come.

I told her the reason behind my panic attack and how I'm much better now. She loves the idea that I'm pregnant but hates how it happens, that's how I feel too but I won't take it out on this child.

We left the building and headed home but stopped to get something to eat on the way there.

After we got our food, we went home and watched a movie while eating.

For the first time in a long time, I finally feel like I don't have to look over my shoulders and that I don't need to worry about anything else.

"I'm going to school tomorrow," I spoke out of nowhere.

She paused the movie, "are you sure about that?"

I nodded my head. "I'm very sure, I missed too much of it and there is something I need to do," I said with a smirk

I saw the confused look on her face, but I wasn't going to tell her anything. I needed to do this first before I can tell her.

I was going to wait to go to school and just go visit her during her office hours but I'm ready to go to school and get this over with.

I started the movie back and laid my head down on Erica's lap. She started rubbing her fingers through my hair and soon after I was falling asleep.

"Come on, get up Lolo. We going to be late." I heard Erica say.

I was feeling way too tired and didn't want to get up, but I did anyway. I dragged myself into the bathroom.

I washed my face and brushed my teeth then jumped into the shower.

Once I got into the shower the cold water woke me up halfway. Now I just need some coffee to finish off the job.

I got out of the shower and dried off. I got dressed and walked out of the room and toward the kitchen.

"Please tell me you made coffee," I whined.

"I did but you can't have any, but I made you hot chocolate." I groan and grab the cup from the table.

"And why can't I have coffee?" I questioned.

"You're pregnant and you have to start thinking about the baby. Coffee is not good for him/her." She said while walking out of the kitchen.

I followed her to the living room with my cup in my hand. I guess she is right, I need to think about the baby now and not just myself.

I finish the hot chocolate and put the cup in the sink to clean later. It wasn't coffee, but it did wake me up a little more.

I grabbed my backpack and headed out the door behind Erica. Nerves were going all through my body, and I didn't know what I was nervous about, it was just school.

Then I started to think about the reason why I wanted to come back to school, and my nerves started getting worst. I took in some deep breaths to calm myself down because I was getting worked up for nothing.

We got to school and headed straight to class because we were a little behind since I didn't want to get out of bed on time.

She opened the door and walked inside, and everyone turned and looked at the door making me freeze in my steps.

"Welcome back." Everyone said at the same time.

I didn't know people noticed that I was gone, I guess some do know who I am.

"Welcome back London, it's good to see you." Professor Smith said with a bright smile causing me to smile back just as big.

I took my seat and gave all my attention to her.

I wasn't paying attention to what she was talking about for the classwork. I was too busy looking at how perfect her body is, and how kissable her lips look. Light from the room shines down on her caramel skin making it seem like she was the only one in the room.

I could watch her all day and night long, I don't know how I went this long without losing my mind over her.

I guess then I wasn't too focused on my feelings for her, I was too worried about what was going on in my life and being afraid of being touched but now I am over that and the person to blame for that is no longer here.

Being over with what happened in my life has given me the courage to focus on my feelings for the first time and I am loving every bit of it.

I was stuck deep off in my mind that I didn't notice she was standing in front of me calling my name.

"London?"

"Y-yes?" I cursed myself for stuttering.

"Is everything okay? The class has been over a few minutes ago."

I looked around the class and saw that everyone was gone. I started cursing Erica out in my head for not pulling me out of my thought and letting me know it was time to leave.

"Yes, I'm okay. I was just stuck in my head thinking." I mumbled.

I looked up into her eyes and her blue eyes pulled me in. It was like looking out into the ocean, admiring its deep blue of it. I never really looked into her eyes before and now that I have, I don't ever want to look away.

She gave me her perfect white teeth smile, and I couldn't help but smile back at her.

"Are you going to just sit here or are you going to head to your next class?" She whispered.

"I-I don't want to go to my next class, so I'll head to the Café and wait for Erica," I whispered back. The happiness in her eyes seems to fade away to sadness.

I grabbed my bag and got up from my seat. I started walking toward the door, but I stopped and turned around.

This is the best time to say what I need to say, or I will never get to say it.

"On second thought I would like to stay here and talk with you." Her eyes shine bright with happiness again and she pulled me a seat up to her desk.

I sat down and stared at her for a while. I wasn't sure how I wanted to start this off, so I just went with what popped into my head first.

"I like you and I have for a while, but with how my life was, I didn't have the courage to say anything."

"I guess I can say that I've been feeling the same way, but you always seem to want to be to yourself, so I never spoke to you about anything but the schoolwork."

She was right about that, before talking with Dr. Morris and before killing my rapist I always wanted to be alone.

"That's true, I was going through something, and it just came to an end but it's still there a little but not as much now." She made a confused look, but she didn't push me to tell her.

"I wanted to ask you on a date that was the reason I came back to school because honestly I'm still not ready to be back, but before you answered that I need to tell you something and I just want you to listen before you ask questions."

She nodded her head and I started telling her everything. I wanted her to know everything that has happened to me. If I wanted to date her, I needed to tell her about my past and not keep any secrets.

After I was done telling her she had a look of anger, hurt, pity, and tears in her eyes. She walked around from her desk and pulled me into a hug. As soon as her arms were around me, I melted into her touch.

It was as if she was the missing piece my life had been missing.

"I'm sorry that this happen to you, and I would love to go on a date with you." She whispered in my ear.

I looked up at her and gave her a big smile. My eyes dropped down to her lips and back up to her eyes.

I can see that she was doing the same thing.

I leaned in closer to her and she started leaning in as well. There were only a few short inches between our lips, and it felt like forever before her lips were on mine.

Once her lips touched mine, I melted even more into her. The kiss was slow and passionate like we both had been waiting for this to happen.

Kissing her soft lips felt like I was kissing a cloud, I deepen the kiss more and pulled her bottom lip between my teeth before biting on it a little. A soft moan was heard from her and that was music to my ears.

Chapter 9

I was sitting on the couch watching Erica walk back and forth after finding out I have a date with our professor over the weekend.

"I can't believe you told her, and most of all I can't believe you were the one who asked for the date!"

I just nodded my head along every time she said something. I didn't see the big deal out of this and she was worked up for no reason.

She stopped pacing and stood there staring at me.

"Oh, I know we need to go shopping for you a new dress!" She yelled while searching for her keys.

I stayed in my spot and watched her like I had been doing. You would have thought I asked Laura to marry me or something by the way she was acting. I asked Professor Smith on a date Monday and now it's Wednesday, so that's been almost 3 days ago.

I still had 3 days until it was time for my date, and I am not going out of this apartment to shop for a damn dress.

"Erica, come sit down with me please," I said in a low voice.

She stopped what she was doing and came to sit next to me. "We still have 3 days to go shopping, right now I am very tired and just want to eat and go to sleep. I promise tomorrow we will go shopping after school." She nodded her head and grabbed her phone to order some food.

The last thing I need is to be nervous about my very first date. At the thought of that my eyes popped open, and I hurried and turned toward Erica.

"Oh My God! Erica, this is my very first date, I have never been on a date before. What do you do on a date?" She started laughing before answering me.

"Just be yourself, that's why she said yes because you are yourself around her. You're going to dinner and a movie everything is going to be just fine."

Okay, nothing to worry about I can be myself, dinner and a movie are good for a first date and maybe I'll take her to that park I loved so much as a kid.

We sat in the living room and watched whatever the T.V. was playing until our food came. I'm glad she ordered egg rolls and fried rice because that's all I want.

When there was a knock on the door she got up and answered it taking the money with her.

I thought she was going to come back with some food, but she came back with a person. I don't remember ordering anything like that.

"Erica, I thought the food was here. Who is this?"

Erica looks like she just saw a ghost from Christmas past and wouldn't look me in the eye.

"Who are you?" I asked her since my best friend couldn't use her damn mouth.

"I'm Erin, Erica's girlfriend." She spoke.

I believe my eyes are going to hit the floor if they pop open like this again.

"Her what? I don't believe I heard you right."

"I'm her girlfriend? You must be London; she tells me so much about you."

I turned my head and looked at my best friend who can't seem to bring herself to look at me. I stood up from the couch and looked from my best friend to this Erin girl.

"For how long have you two been dating?" I asked them both, but Erin seems to be the only one that was talking.

"It will be 2 years tomorrow, that's why I'm here. A day before our anniversary we would pick which house to come to, so we can wake up together the next day." I listen to her talk while I was staring at the person who is supposed to be my best friend.

"You've been dating someone for 2 years and not once have you told me about them. Not only that, but you have also been dating a girl. Did you not trust me enough to tell me?" I said with hurt in my voice and tears starting to come to my eyes.

I didn't even wait for her to answer my question I turned around and walked toward the room I claimed as mine. I'm glad that she went and got my car from my old place.

I packed a bag and grabbed my keys and phone. I don't care if I was overthinking this, I am hurt by the fact that she couldn't trust me with something as little as this when I trusted her with everything that went on in my life.

I left out of the room to find them still standing in the same spot I left them. I shook my head and walked past them.

"P-please Lolo-" I put my hand up cutting her off.

"I don't want to hear it, Erica," I said and left out the door going toward my car.

I got in and started the car up heading out of the apartment. I pulled over when I was far enough and looked through my phone to find the other person, I felt comfortable with. I found her number and called.

"Hello."

"Hey, it's me."

"I know it's you, my love. What are you doing?"

"S-sitting inside my car." I stuttered out.

"What's wrong?"

"I-um, I know our date is not until Saturday, but can I come over."

"Sure, I'll text you the address."

I hung up after she sent me her address, I put it into the GPS and started my car back up.

It didn't take long to get to her house from where I was, and I was glad about that because I don't like driving while upset.

It's crazy because I never got this upset at Erica before. I never had a reason to be upset with her. I trusted her with everything, and I thought she did too, but I guess I was wrong about that.

I parked my car and got out leaving my bag inside. I didn't have any plans of staying the night here I just wanted to be in her arms.

I walked up to her door and knocked a few times and waited until the door was pulled open.

I gave a weak smile and hugged her tight feeling some of the anger leave my body.

She hugged me just as tight before pulling me inside the house and closing the door behind me.

"Now tell me what's wrong." I nodded my head and followed her into the living room.

I sat down on the couch and started telling her what happened at Erica's place. In the middle of telling her my phone started to ring and I looked down to see that it was Erica. I sent it to the voice mail and finish telling Laura what happened.

"I thought we trusted each other but I guess it was one-way."

"Maybe she was afraid of how you would react," Laura said.

"I don't believe it because before I even told her how I felt about you or before I even dated a girl I told her that I was into women. She could have told me then, but she still didn't say anything."

My phone started to ring again but this time it wasn't Erica, it was a different number that I didn't know. I wasn't going to answer it, but Laura picked it up and answered it herself.

I didn't pay attention to who she was talking to or what they were talking about. I just felt hurt that my best friend who I thought was my sister couldn't trust me with something as simple as this.

No matter what or who she liked I still would have been there for her. I still would have loved her the same as I always did, but she should know that once you break my trust it's hard to get it back.

She was the only person I had that was close to family and I feel like I lost that by something as little as this.

I felt hands wrap around my waist pulling me out of my thought. I looked up at Laura and gave her a smile that I'm sure didn't reach my eyes.

I let her pull me onto her lap and I place my head on her shoulders while wrapping my arms around her neck.

"It's going to be okay my love, once you have calmed down talk to her and give her a chance to explain." I nodded my head but knowing me it was going to be a little minute before I spoke to her again.

Erica

Once she left out of the door, I couldn't help the tears that came. I watched my only sister leave and who knows when she will come back or talk to me again.

I don't know why I didn't tell her; I could have told her when she told me about her being gay, but I didn't say anything.

Erin pulled me into her and hugged me tight and I hugged back the same while letting the tears fall.

"I'm sorry babe, I didn't know you haven't told her." She whispered.

It's not her fault I don't blame her, London had to find out someday and today was that day.

"I-I can't lose her Erin, she's my only sister and I know I'm her only sister as well." I cried out.

I let go of Erin and tried to call London, but she kept sending me to the voice mail.

"Give me your phone," I told her, and once she did, I called London praying that she would answer it.

When it was getting close to the last ring, I was starting to lose hope until I heard someone answer.

"London?"

"No, this is not London who's calling?"

"This is Erica, I need to speak to London."

"Sorry Erica, this is Professor Smith. London won't get the phone and I thought you would try from another number to get her to answer but give her time and let her calm down I promise to tell her to call you."

I nodded my head forgetting that she couldn't see me. "Okay, thank you." I hung up the phone and gave it back to Erin.

She didn't want to talk to me and knowing that Professor Smith promised to have her call me back, but I know that's not going to happen.

I looked up to Erin with more tears in my eyes not knowing what else to do but waiting until Lolo feel okay with talking with me again.

Erin came over to the couch and pulled me into her lap hugging me tightly.

"I-I can't lose her." I cried.

Chapter 10

London

Laying down on the couch with my head resting on her stomach and her fingers running through my hair makes all the tension in my body go away.

Thinking back to why I came over here made me snuggle more into her.

I know I may have overdone things, but I felt like part of my friendship with Erica was a lie. If I knew that she was into women, I would have never been so scared of how she would react to me coming out.

Feeling the tears slide down my face I try to stop them before Laura notices them. Crying is one thing but crying in front of someone is another story, it makes me feel weak all over again.

I felt her wrap her arms around me and hugged me tight against her.

"It's going to be okay love." She whispered.

I nodded my head and closed my eyes feeling tired from all the useless crying I had been doing.

"I think you should call her and let her explain." I heard Laura say.

I sigh and nod my head agreeing with her. I do need to call her and get an answer from her. I need to know why she felt like she couldn't tell me.

I sat up and grabbed my phone from the table that Laura sat it on.

"I'll go make us something to eat." She said while getting up.

Once she left out of the living room, I called Erica.

"Lolo?!"

I didn't say anything for a minute because I didn't know what to say or how to say it.

"Yeah, it's me."

"I'm glad you called back Lolo."

She has been calling me that since the first time we met in 10th grade.

"I just want to know why you felt like you couldn't tell me." I heard her sigh before she started talking.

"I didn't tell you because I didn't know how you would feel about it and I didn't want to lose you as my best friend, my sister."

"Why didn't you tell me when I came out to you?"

"That was your time and I just wanted to be there for you. I was going to tell you the day I got that phone call then I had to wait again because you needed me, and I didn't want anything to be about me."

I guess she has a point there, maybe she did want to tell me but didn't have the right chance to do so.

"I'm sorry Lolo, I didn't mean to make you upset. I should have just come out with it please don't leave me." She cried out the last part which broke my heart.

"It's okay, I'm not going anywhere you're my sister and my only family but I'm not coming home tonight or tomorrow."

"Why not?"

"That's the time you need with your girlfriend plus I'm at Laura's."

"But what about the doctor's appointment tomorrow?"

"I'll go from here, don't worry about going to this one there will be many more you can go to."

After I finish talking with Erica, we said our goodbyes and I got up off the couch to go into the kitchen.

I stood there watching her cook, admiring everything about her.

"You know it's rude to stare." She said without looking up at me.

I giggled and walked over to the table to have a seat.

"Erica and I made up with everything."

She turned around and smiled at me. I gave her one back before going through my phone to see what time I need to be at the appointment.

Sadly, I would be going by myself because it's a school day and I can't just ask Laura to go with me when I know she has a class she needs to teach.

"What's on your mind?"

"Nothing," I mumble my reply.

"With that face, it's more than nothing." She said back to me.

I sighed and looked up at her, "I have a doctor's appointment tomorrow and I will be going by myself."

"Why are you going by yourself?"

"I told Erica not to worry about going with me since her girlfriend is at the house with her."

I started playing a game on my phone trying to get my mind to slow down from all the thinking I have been doing these past few weeks.

"I'll come with you."

I snapped my head up to her and shook my head no. "I can't ask you to do that because I know you have a class to teach."

"I'll call and cancel the class for tomorrow, I want to be there for you London." She said while walking over to me and standing between my legs.

I wrapped my arms around her waist and looked up at her giving her the biggest smile that came across my face. "Thanks," I said and hugged her tight.

She went back over to the stove and finish cooking dinner. Not long after the food was ready, and she was bringing the plates over to the table.

I thanked her and waited for her to come back with drinks before starting to eat.

My mouth watered from the amazing taste of this pasta she made, it tasted like heaven on a plate.

"This is amazing, you have to teach me how to make it." She smiled and nodded her head.

We talked about any and everything. We talked about the plans after I finish school. I wanted to start looking for a job right after I finish school, but I don't know if I should wait now and wait for the baby to be born or should I just go with the plan I had put together already.

I can't believe I'm going to be a mom, I never thought that I would ever have kids. Honestly, kids were never part of my future other than teaching them at some high school.

Sometimes things never go as planned and God has other things planned out for you.

I felt something warm and welcoming, so I snuggled closer to it falling back into a deep sleep.

"Come on love it's time to get up." I heard but I still wasn't about to get up I was too comfortable.

I felt light kisses going all over my face and down my neck making me giggle.

"Okay, I'm up," I whined.

"I'll go and get some breakfast cooked and you get showered and dressed."

"Wait, I left my bag in the car." I stretched out my body and got up about to leave out the room.

"You get in the shower, and I'll get the bag." I smiled at her and headed toward her bathroom.

This is still something I need to get used to, the only person I'm used to showing me love like this is Erica and that's because she is the only one, I trust.

I turned the shower on warm and got undressed getting inside it. The warm water fell down my body and I let out a sigh.

Before starting to wash up I placed my hand over my belly. 'I don't know how I'm going to do it little one but no matter what I'll always have you.'

I finally started washing my body and hair. After I was done, I wrapped a towel around my body and hair stepping out of the bathroom.

I notice my bag sitting next to the bed, I walked over and start grabbing my clothes.

I put on my underwear and started working on my hair. I didn't feel like doing it, so I just put it up in a messy bun.

Once I was fully dressed, I left out of her room and headed downstairs going straight to the kitchen.

"I am so hungry," I whined.

I heard Laura giggle and then turned to face me, "I just finish with breakfast."

"Did you make pancakes?" I question with a hopeful look.

"Yes, go have a seat and I'll bring your food over to you." I nodded my head and kissed her cheek before going to take my seat.

When she brought me my food, I didn't eat anything but the pancakes. Everything else made me feel like I was going to be sick. I pushed the plate over to her.

"I think I'm going to be sick." Soon as those words left my mouth I was running toward the bathroom.

I made it just in time. I felt Laura rub her hand on my back.

"Morning sickness is a bitch," I said once I was done.

"I know love, you'll get past it soon."

I sat on the floor and Laura grabbed a face rag and cleaned my face before handing me a toothbrush with toothpaste already on it.

I brushed my teeth and fix myself back up hoping that this morning sickness is done for the day.

I looked at the time and saw that it was getting close to the time of my appointment.

I grabbed my purse and made sure I had everything in it and that I wouldn't need to go back to Erica's apartment for anything.

I was going to drive my car, but Laura wanted to drive and honestly, I didn't feel like driving anyways.

I told her where we needed to go, and I let the seat back some and closed my eyes. I was not liking being pregnant already. Feeling sleepy all the damn time and throwing up whatever you just ate, it's a living hell.

Not long after we were pulling up to the place, I felt my nerves take a turn for the worst. I don't know what I was nervous about, but I was.

Now I wish I did tell Erica to come with me.

We got out of the car and headed straight into the building and up to the front desk.

"Appointment for London Wilson," I told the lady.

She started typing on her computer, you could tell she didn't want to be there because not once did she smile.

"Just have a seat and the doctor will be right with you."

I nodded my head and grabbed Laura's hand leading her to the waiting area.

"Lolo, finally you made it here." I turned around to see Erica and her girlfriend standing there.

I ran up to her and hugged her tight, you would have thought we haven't seen each other in a lifetime but fighting with her and leaving made it feel like it was.

"What are you doing here?" I asked.

"I couldn't miss the first appointment of my god baby." Was her simple answer.

Chapter 11

I was surprised that Erica and her girlfriend Erin were here at my appointment, I thought they would have been out somewhere since it's their 2nd anniversary.

"I thought you both would have been out doing something other than being here waiting for god knows how long for me to see the doctor."

"We were going to go out on a date, but I just couldn't miss this appointment plus Erin wanted to be here too," Erica said.

I looked over to Erin and gave her a small smile. I need to apologize to her for how I handled things. It wasn't her fault that Erica didn't tell me, but I still feel like I took things out on her.

I walked up to her with this small smile on my face, "I'm sorry about how I handle things I didn't mean to take them out on you."

"It's not a big deal, I would have done the same thing too if my best friend kept that kind of secret." She pulled me into a hug, and I tensed up at first before relaxing into her touch.

I'm starting to get used to people touching me, but it's still a working process.

We all took our seats with me sitting next to Laura and Erica next to Erin which puts us in the middle.

I grabbed Laura's hand and gave her a smile as a way of thanking her for doing this with me. She knew what I was doing and nodded her head giving me a smile in return.

We sat and talked with each other while waiting for my name to be called. I got to know Erin a little bit and Erica got to know Laura a little as well.

It was a little weird for a minute because Erica kept calling her professor, but I think she was doing that on purpose.

"London Wilson." We were in the middle of talking when we heard my name being called.

I looked up and saw the doctor standing there waiting for me to get up. Once I got up everyone else did as well. We followed her into one of the back rooms.

I didn't know what she was going to do since it was my first doctor's appointment and well my first time being pregnant.

"Here, change into this and I'll be right back."

She gave me a hospital gown and I notice there was no privacy curtain in here.

"Okay, you three need to turn around," I said while pushing them to turn the other way.

"Damn thought I was going to get a show." I heard Laura say and we all bust out laughing.

I hurried and changed into the gown and sat down on the bed. "I'm done."

"Finally, I thought I was going to have to look at the wall all day long," Erica said.

We laughed at how she was being dramatic. Not long after the doctor came back in with a folder in her hand that had my name on it.

"Hello, I'm Dr. White and I'll be your doctor until this little sunshine is born." She said with nothing but joy in her voice.

You can tell that she enjoyed doing her job because that smile on her face never left once.

She had me lay back on the bed while she did all the things she needed to do.

"Okay, everything is fine so far. Your heart rate is great but I'm a little worried about your blood pressure, so I am putting you on a light salt diet." I nodded my head, the only thing I eat with a lot of salt is chips.

"Now let's check on your little one."

I watched as she went to the machine and started tapping on buttons. After she walked back over to me with a bottle of gel I'm guessing.

"This is going to be cold for a moment." I nodded my head but got chills after she places the gel on my stomach.

She started rubbing it around with something that I don't know the name of it. I looked at the screen to see what was going on, but I didn't understand what I was supposed to be looking at or for.

She pointed to a small dot on the screen, and I looked in closer. "That little dot right there is your baby."

I couldn't help the smile that came across my face and the joy that I was feeling inside my body.

This little dot on the screen is my baby and will grow even bigger.

"In a few months you'll be able to hear the heartbeat, it's the most amazing sound for a mother to hear." She spoke. I looked up at her and gave her a big smile. I can't wait to be able to hear the heartbeat of my baby.

"I wish we were able to hear it now, but I take it the baby still needs to grow and everything needs to form," Erica said, and the doctor nodded her head.

I let them ask the doctor questions as I went off into my mind thinking and rubbing on my belly that will be bigger in 9 months. No matter how this little one got into this world I am still going to love him/her with every part of me.

I felt someone's hand wipe my face and I looked up to see that it was Laura standing on the side of me.

She leaned over and whispered in my ear, "what's wrong love?"

"Thinking about how this child got here, and how I'm still going to love him/her with everything in me."

The doctor wiped the gel off my stomach and had me get back dressed.

We finish talking about everything that I need to be doing to have a great birth. She told me to get some vitamins to take every day. To make sure I walk every chance I get and eat healthily.

It is so much you need to do to make sure you have a healthy baby, and I am willing to do anything to make sure my baby comes out healthy.

I had to go to the front and speak with that nurse again who seems to have a stick up her ass. I got another appointment that was two weeks from now.

"Okay, I'm hungry now," I told them, and they all started laughing like I was joking.

I glared at them and that shut them up quick.

"Damn she's scary when pregnant." I heard Erica say and Erin agreed with her. I take it Laura was taking the safe way out and not saying anything at all.

"What do you want to eat?" Laura asked me.

"I want some pizza and wings. Can we get some?" I asked her while looking into her eyes. She nodded her head and smiled at me before kissing my lips.

"Anything for you, my love."

Having lunch with my best friend, her girlfriend, and Laura made me smile a real smile that I didn't know I still had in me.

It felt nice being around other people and not having to worry about anything or anyone. I felt like I can be myself, but I'm still trying to understand who I am.

After we had lunch Erica and Erin went on about their day while Laura and I went back to her house. I needed to get my things and head back home tonight even though I don't want to. When I slept next to her, I woke up feeling relaxed and at peace without a dream in the world last night.

I couldn't ask to stay the night again because I know she needs her space, and I didn't want to be a bother.

I was lost in my head that I didn't know we had made it back to her house until she shook me a little while calling my name.

"You okay there? I have been calling you." She asked with worry in her voice.

"Yes, I'm okay just got caught up in my head again," I said while opening the door to get out of the car.

I waited by the door for her and when she opened the door I walked in and headed straight to her living room laying across her couch. This couch is very comfortable that I can sleep on it every night.

She came over and lifted my head before sitting down. I looked up at her and smiled at her.

Just looking into her beautiful eyes gives me chills, hope, and happiness. Every little detail about her makes her seem special in all kinds of ways that I can't put my finger on it.

Out of everyone in this world, I'm glad my heart picked her to trust, love, and be happy with but I'm not ready to say that I love her.

Chapter 12

I have been back home for a few days now and everything is back to the way they're supposed to be but with Erin here more these days.

I like Erin, she makes my best friend happy and I'm glad that Erica has someone that makes her smile the way Laura makes me.

Thinking about her always brings a smile to my face, she is on her way to pick me up for our very first date and I'm a little nervous about it.

I have never been on a date before but what Erica and Erin told me makes it seem very easy to get through. I mean I just need to be myself whoever the hell that is.

Taking in some deep breaths I finish getting ready and by the time I was done, there was a knock at the door, and Erica running to it like she was a 5year old trying to beat someone else to the door.

I heard her and Erin gasp at the same time causing me to leave out of my room with my purse in my hand.

Looking at the door I gasp myself staring at the goddess that's standing before us. How in the hell can someone look that damn good without trying?

"That's not even fair, I put so much work into my everyday routine and I never come out of the house looking like this." I heard Erica say causing all of us to laugh.

Walking up to Laura and giving her a quick kiss on the cheek and pulling back smiling up at her, "You look beautiful."

"You look beautiful yourself. Ready to go?" I nodded my head and waved bye to the couple that's going to have the house to themselves tonight.

She opened the door for me, and I gave her a quick thank you before getting in and allowing her to close the door behind me.

Putting my seat belt on and looking over to her asking her where we were going but it's been the same answer all day since I been asking, 'it's a surprise.' I shook my head and looked out the window watching the other cars pass by.

Feeling her hand grab mine and hold it while she was driving made me smile. I notice that she did this during the time she took me to my appointment and whenever we were at lunch, she would just touch me.

I think it's a physical thing for her. I like it though it made me feel wanted by someone and how they need me just as much as I need them.

Not long after we pulled up to a restaurant, I always wanted to try but never had the guts to go to, plus it was one of those restaurants you took your lover to. I looked over at her and gave her the biggest smile that came across my face.

"I always wanted to come here," I said to her as I reached over and hugged her.

"I know, I might have asked Erica about something you always wanted to do, and she told me about this place." I smiled at her again and we both got out of the car.

I waited for her to lock up the car and we walked into the restaurant holding hands. When we got inside, I was amazed at how it looked, every wall looked like it was made of glass. Each table was set for a couple and some table was set for more people.

Tables with people sitting at them had flowers and candles going, with a white tablecloth and gold chairs. The lights were set perfectly giving that romantic vibe in the room.

"Table for two under Laura Smith." I heard Laura say bringing my attention back to her and the waiter.

"Right this way ladies."

We followed the waiter toward our table, and I was hoping that one of the tables that I was looking at not long ago was one of ours, but I was wrong because we bypassed each one of them.

Soon we came into a room that had low music playing in the background and the lights were set just like the room we left out of but there was only one table.

"Welcome to the VIP room. Your waiter will be right with you." The guy said before walking away.

Laura pulled out the chair for me and I took it while still looking at her. This room by itself must cost a nice amount.

"You didn't have to do this."

"I know I didn't, but you deserve nothing but the best and it's my way of thanking you for letting me be the first to take you on a date."

I felt my face getting hot and my heart starting to beat fast. She is right this is my first date and I'm glad that I picked her to be the one to take me on it.

"Welcome to the Lover's room, I'm Den and I'll be your waiter for tonight what can I start you off with." The waiter said.

"A bottle of red wine and two glasses of water." Laura did the talking which I was happy about. I'm not a drinker but a glass of wine won't hurt for tonight.

He left leaving us alone once again in this beautiful room that I cannot get tired of.

I started playing with my fingers getting nervous because I didn't know what to say or how to act on this date. I felt Laura's hands come down on top of mine causing me to look up at her into her light blue ocean eyes.

Her eyes alone pull my heart this way and that way, and I could never understand why.

"Nothing to be nervous about just be yourself." She spoke with a soft tone of voice.

I smiled and nodded my head feeling the nerves leave my body.

"What made you want to teach?" I asked randomly.

"I like learning new and different things about English, and I always wanted to share that with others, so what better way to do that than teach. I also love to write and spend my free time reading all kinds of different books."

I love writing and reading myself and English is the best way to go when you love something like this.

"What about you? I know that's what you're going to school for."

"I like to write, I feel as though you can express yourself through the words you write or type," I whispered to her knowing that's what I did the whole time before she knew about my life.

I looked into her eyes, and they turned sad for a moment and left the next. If I wasn't looking at her, I would have missed it.

"I wish I knew you were trying to reach out and that your stories weren't just stories." She whispered while reaching over to take my hand.

During those days I wish I did have the guts to speak up about my need for help, but I couldn't, and I didn't know why.

I went to say something, but the waiter came with our wine and water, we weren't ready to order because we haven't even looked at the menu yet.

I didn't know what to order everything looked amazing and pricey.

"I'm not sure what to get, what are you going with?" I asked her while putting my menu back down.

"I think I am going with the steak dinner, and I think you should try this chicken dinner with the veggies."

That doesn't sound so bad, I think she picked that because it says light salt and it has veggies which I am okay with.

Not long after we agreed on what to order the waiter came and took our orders and we got back to talking about school and what I'm going to do after I finish. I still need to think about that because I have a little one to think about now.

She had me laughing and smiling, and it felt good to be able to do something like this and I was loving every moment of it. I never thought someone can smile so much but now I see that it's true.

"I love hearing you laugh and seeing you smile; it makes my day and night always." She said randomly making me give her another smile I was trying to hide.

Our food came, and we begin eating. The food was amazing, but Laura's food looked better than mine I wanted some, but I wasn't going to be greedy. I think it's because I'm pregnant and my cravings are going crazy.

I took another bite of my food and pushed the rest to the side which was half the plate.

"Is everything okay?" She asked.

I shook my head no and started looking at the floor. I felt so greedy, but this craving was killing me, and I just wanted her plate, well the rest of it.

"What's wrong." She asked again.

I pointed at her food, and she looked down and back up at me giving me a smile that could brighten up a whole room.

She put some on the fork and started feeding it to me, and God it tasted so damn amazing and I wanted more which she did give me.

I felt better after I ate her food, and she finishes mine. I only had one glass of wine because I am pregnant and don't want to hurt the baby.

After she paid the bill which she wouldn't let me see. We grabbed our things and left out.

We walked toward the car while talking. No matter what it is I can talk to her about it and I like that.

She opened the door for me, and I thanked her while getting inside. I never knew people were this nice.

I didn't want the night to end but I didn't want to go anywhere else either. I think she knew that as well because not long after we were pulling up to her house.

We got out of the car and walked up to her house when she unlocked the door letting us in the warmth in this house felt like home and I loved it.

I followed her upstairs toward her room to change out of this damn dress and heels. She helped me out of the dress and her fingers slowly brushed up against my back causing me to get chills.

Her touch felt so welcoming, and I wanted more but I knew I wasn't ready for that part yet. She kissed my shoulder and then my ear before whispering into it. "When you're ready my love I will show you how your body should be treated and taken care of."

I was lost for words and all I was able to do was nod my head before I went back to changing into the oversize t-shirt, she gave me.

She went into the closet and changed herself coming back out in the same thing as me.

I climbed into her bed and waited for her to turn everything off and turn the T.V. on.

She climbed into bed once she did and turned on a movie. I snuggled closer to her laying my head on her chest and watching the movie.

Her fingers started massaging my scalp and I felt myself dozing off from the feeling.

This was the best way to end our night and I would do it all over again with her, giving her my first everything.

Chapter 13

I jumped from my sleep and ran into the bathroom heading for the toilet, I tried my best to be quiet and not wake Laura, but I don't think I did a good job with that because I push the door into the wall letting it make a loud sound.

I don't know how much more of this I can take, waking up in the middle of the night throwing up and then turning around trying to eat everything.

Feeling something rub on my back I looked up to see Laura standing there with worry all over her face. I turned back around trying to hide from her not wanting her to see me like this.

I heard the water going and not long after I felt her pulling my face toward her and wiping my mouth. I gave a small smile before going to brush my teeth.

After I finish brushing my teeth, I followed her back out into the room and got into bed. I snuggled closer to her and laid my head on her chest. She wrapped her arms around me and pulled me even closer.

Being in her arms I feel even safer.

We laid in bed with nothing but silence, not a bad silence but a silence we could both think in.

I looked over at the clock and saw that it was 5 in the morning, and I was hungry.

"Can we get something to eat?" I whispered into her ear.

"At this time of morning love?" I nodded my head and waited for an answer.

"I'm not sure if anything is open but I can make you something if you like." I nodded my head to that idea. I love her cooking.

She got out of bed, and I followed her downstairs even though she told me to stay in bed. I sat in the living room watching whatever was on the T.V. when I turned it on.

The food was smelling amazing, but I was starting to get sleepy again. I wanted to fight it, but it was getting hard to fight my sleep, so I let myself doze off.

I don't know how long I had been sleeping but I heard Laura calling my name while she was shaking me to get me up. I didn't know I was that tired and still am.

I woke up and smiled at her. "I didn't mean to go to sleep."

"It's okay love I know you're tired." She whispered back to me.

I grabbed the hand she had held out to me allowing her to help me off the couch and into the kitchen. I smiled when I walked into the kitchen seeing that she made a big breakfast for just us and even better she made pancakes.

I sat down at the table waiting for her to take her seat as well before I started eating. She grabbed us some orange juice and took her seat across from me. I believe this is something I can get used to.

We started eating breakfast and having small talk with her eating the things on my plate I'm not going to eat.

Honestly, I just wanted the pancakes which I ate mine and hers. I was full and ready to sleep some more, but she had other plans for us.

"Come on let's go get showered and dressed. The doctor said you need to walk a lot while you're pregnant." I nodded my head to her and dragged myself away from the table and up the stairs with her following behind me.

Grabbing the clothes from my overnight bag and headed toward the shower to jump in for a quick shower since I'm not really in the mood to do anything today.

Taking my quick shower, I washed my body and hair with her body wash and shampoo.

I got out of the shower and dried myself off along with my hair. I'll just let it be curly for today.

Putting on my black jeans and tank top, I walked out of the bathroom to see Laura coming back into the room.

"Ready to head out?" She asked me. I gave her a look that said not really but you're making me.

"Come on don't give me that look you need to do some walking." I sigh and grab my jacket following her out of the room.

"Can we stop by the apartment first? I want to see Erica." I asked her while she locked up the house.

She nodded her head and helped me into the car. It's very sweet that people still do this with the one they love or like. I didn't think anyone did this still and I love it.

Ugh, I fell asleep again and she doesn't even live that far from Erica. How can someone fall asleep that fast?

"I'm tired of being tired. I don't even know if that made any sense."

"I understand what you mean and it's normal with being pregnant." I nodded my head and got out of the car. I looked around to see if Erica was there, once I saw her car I rushed to her apartment and knocked.

I know I have a key, but I wanted her to come to the door. I know I'm lazy but who cares.

Once I heard the door unlock, I started bouncing on my feet. I have only been gone since last night, but I still miss her, I think it's my hormones messing with me.

When she opened the door, I jumped into her arms and wrapped my legs around her waist, like I haven't seen her in days when it's only been one night.

"Well, I missed you too Lolo, but it's only been one night."

"I don't care I missed you and you're my best friend and I have the right to miss you," I whined in her ear.

She laughed at me before putting me back down on my feet and greeting Laura who was laughing at me as well.

I didn't think it was funny and it was starting to hurt my feelings. I think my hormones are getting the best of me and I can't turn them off.

I didn't know I was crying until Erica wiped my face and looked at me with worry written all over her face.

"What's wrong honey?" She asked.

"It's not funny that you're both laughing at me, and I don't know why I am even crying and I just can't stop these damn tears for some reason and I'm fucking hungry again and I just ate." I sobbed out.

I didn't think being pregnant would make me this damn emotional. Who would want to get pregnant just to be damn emotional? I damn sure wish this shit would be over with already.

Laura pulled me into her and wrapped me in her arms and hugged me close to her making all the emotions wash away.

I let out a sigh and hugged her back and allowed her to wipe the tears from my face.

"Now can I have some food before I lose my fucking mind?"

"We just ate how can you still be hungry?" Laura asked.

I looked back at her and my eyes started getting watery again. "Are you calling me fat? I'm not even showing yet and you calling me fat already." I cried out.

"No, no that's not what I'm saying, love. You're beautiful and you're nowhere near fat and you going to be even more beautiful when you start showing. You can have as much food as you would like." I nodded my head and wipe my face and walked into the house leaving them two at the door.

I walked into the kitchen to see what was in there to eat. I noticed a pizza box on the stove and grabbed a slice out of the box. I started eating it while walking back into the living room where everyone else was at.

"Hi, Erin." I greeted with a mouth full.

"Hi to you too London." She said with a smile on her face.

It's nice knowing Erica has someone that will love her and make her happy, my best friend's happiness means everything to me.

There wasn't much room on the couch, so I sat on Laura's lap and went back to eating the pizza I took from the kitchen.

We were watching what they had on the T.V. before we came, and it looked good, but I didn't want to watch a movie.

I looked back at them, and they were into the movie.

"I want to go to the mall and since you made me come out of the house that's what we're going to do," I told Laura.

She only nodded her head and asked them if they wanted to come as well. Erica didn't take long to answer since she likes to shop, but Erin didn't seem to like the idea of shopping.

We all left the house and got into Laura's car. I didn't see a reason to take two different cars when we all are going to the same place.

Laura and I went off looking at different stores for baby clothes. They all were so cute, and I just wanted to buy them all and so did Laura. I like how she's okay with going out with me even though I'm pregnant.

I'm not sure where things will go with us, but I do hope they go somewhere, and she will be a part of my future with my child.

Chapter 14

I swear it doesn't feel like it's been a month already since I been pregnant and since my first appointment, not only that it's been a month since me and Laura been dating, and it's been the best month of my life.

I never thought being around someone can make you this happy and that you will always want to be around them no matter what. I'm just surprised she still wants to be around me with those mood swings I keep having and waking up in the middle of the night wanting something to eat.

Most of my days are spent here with her when I don't want to be around Erica and Erin. I love them both but they both drive me crazy.

Being here feels like home and I never want to leave here, and I think she knows that too.

Right now, I am getting ready while she is making something for breakfast. She wanted to take me to my appointment again, I think she is getting attached to the baby as well.

Every night before we go to sleep, she would lay her head close to my stomach and read to the baby, I think it's the sweetest thing ever and I can never thank her enough for doing what she is doing.

Once I finish getting ready, I left out of the room and headed downstairs toward the kitchen where I smelled the food coming from.

I walked into the kitchen to see Laura making herself a cup of coffee which I am jealous about because I can't have any.

"I want some so bad," I whined while looking at her cup. She shook her head and handed me a cup of orange juice which I thanked her for.

"Pancakes ready, since I know that's all you wanted." I smiled at her and kissed her on the cheek before taking my seat at the dinner table.

I started stuffing my face with pancakes making sure not to get it on my clothes.

Feeling that she is staring at me I looked up at her with my mouth full of food. I finish eating what was in my mouth before speaking, "yes?" I questioned.

"Nothing, I'm just taking in your beauty."

I could feel my face getting hot and the nerves in my stomach jumping around like crazy. I smiled at her and finish eating my food.

After I was done eating, I cleaned myself up and waited for her to get her things together as well.

She unlocked the car while she was locking up the house, so I went and got into the car waiting for her. Normally she would wait to unlock the car, so she can open the door for me. I guess she didn't want me waiting on my feet long.

Soon she was in the car starting it up and pulling off from in front of her house. I notice I didn't have morning sickness today and I smiled at that because I was getting tired of eating for it to come right back up.

"I notice you didn't get sick this morning." I heard Laura say.

I didn't know she was paying that much attention to me, but I like that she is, it lets me know that she cares about me.

"Yeah, I noticed that as well, I'm glad I didn't get sick this morning," I said with a smile.

After that, there was silence in the car, but you could hear the soft sound of the music playing on the radio.

10 minutes later we were pulling up to my doctor's office. I sigh and get out of my seat belt. I waited for Laura to come on my side of the car, so I could hold her hand something I grew to like doing.

Some of the students and Professors found out about us and they're happy that we are dating, I even found out that she has been liking me for a long time. I thought that was sweet.

We walked into the building heading up to the front desk hoping that there will be a new assistant this time.

When we made it to the front desk there was a new face sitting behind the desk.

"Hello, I have an appointment today with Dr. White," I said to the lady.

"Name please." She said with a smile.

"London Wilson."

She started typing on her computer, I guess checking me in for my appointment.

"Okay, have a seat and the doctor will be with you soon." I thanked her and walked over to the waiting area with Laura right behind me.

I looked around the waiting room and saw other soon-to-be moms with their lovers or friend. I smiled at the sight and looked back over to Laura with that same smile still on my face.

"What's got you smiling like that?"

"All these soon-to-be moms in here with their lover or friend. I know the way I got pregnant is the wrong way and it will forever be with me, but I can never take that out on this little bundle of joy, and I have you by my side which makes everything so much better." I said with a smile.

We talked for a little bit before my name was called. I grabbed her hand and walked toward Dr. White who was waiting for us.

I greeted her with a smile and got the same in return.

We followed her to a room that looks the same as the last one when I had my first appointment.

I sat on the bed and Laura sat in the chair by the bed. Once again, I had to put on this damn gown, but lucky me I wore a dress today.

This time I didn't care if she saw me changing because she sees it back at home. Home? I smiled at that thought, I would love to call her place home.

Passing her my dress I put the gown on and got back into the bed.

The doctor came back five minutes later giving me enough time to make myself comfortable.

"Okay, you are now a month pregnant, and this is your second appointment, right?" I nodded my head and finish listening to her talk.

"Let's go ahead and give you a checkup."

It didn't take long for her to give me this checkup. My heart rate was good, my blood pressure was better than the last time and I'm very happy.

"Whatever you are doing keep it up, your blood pressure is looking amazing and didn't scare me this time." I giggled at the doctor with her fake acting.

"I have Laura to thank for that, she won't let me eat anything that's not good for me or the baby," I tell the doctor while staring at my lover.

"Well, thank you, momma, for making sure she eats healthy."

I noticed Laura's eyes popped open and I had to replay what the doctor said and soon my eyes popped open as well.

I didn't know what to say and from the looks of it neither did Laura.

"Let's check and see how the baby is doing." The doctor said.

Doing the only thing I could do, I nodded my head and waited for her to put this cold ass gel on my stomach.

Reaching for Laura's hand to hold because I was nervous about how the baby was doing. I have been feeling pain here and there and I haven't told the doctor yet, but Laura knows.

Feeling the cold gel on my stomach I closed my eyes to get myself used to the feeling of the gel.

"Okay, let's see can we find the little one."

I opened my eyes and looked at the screen that will show the baby, it looked a little weird. I mean who wanted to see the inside of their stomach for 9 months.

"There we go. The baby is growing healthy as it should." I nodded my head.

"When will we be able to hear the heartbeat?" Laura asked.

"After she is five months pregnant, but you will be able to hear it when she is six months."

She cleaned the gel off my stomach and allowed me to sit up.

"Is there anything you would like to know before we end this appointment?" She asked us.

"She's been having a little pain lately is that something we should worry about," Laura asked.

"Not at all, all first-time moms go through something like this, but if that pain gets worse come in and we'll have a look to see what is going on." Dr. White said to Laura.

"When can we find out the sex of the baby?" I questioned.

I wanted to know because I wanted to start shopping like crazy and I knew Laura, Erica, and Erin wanted to shop as well.

"We can find out now by doing a blood test." She spoke.

Not thinking twice about it I let her take some blood from me. Once she was done, I got dressed and we went out into the waiting room to wait for the test to come back.

I leaned on Laura, and she placed her arm around me pulling me closer to her.

"How did that make you feel?" She asked out of nowhere.

"How did what make me feel?" I respond with a question.

"That she called me your child's momma."

I smiled up at her, "it made me feel happy that she thought you were the mom. I mean I would like that a lot, but I wouldn't ask you to do something like that."

"Before I say something back to that there is something I want to ask you first." I nodded my head and waited for her to ask me what she needed to ask.

"I know it's only been a month since we were dating, but you stay at my house more than you do at Erica's. I'm not sure where things are going but I do know where I want them to go." She took a deep breath and looked at me.

"I want to make things official with us, so London Wilson will you be my girlfriend?"

I'm sure the smile on my face is big as ever and it's starting to hurt my face, but I didn't care. I have been waiting for her to ask me this for a month now and she finally did.

Jumping from my seat into her lap I wrapped my arms around her neck while saying yes over again.

"I waited for this and you're finally doing it. It took you long enough." I giggled in her ear.

"Well, I wanted to do it over dinner tonight, but things never go as planned when it comes down to life."

She was right, nothing ever goes to plan when it comes down to life things just happened when they are ready to happen.

We waited another hour before Dr. White called me back again with the results in her hand.

Before getting up and going toward the doctor I looked up at Laura.

"What do you think it will be?"

"I'm hoping it's a boy." She smiled.

"I'm hoping it's a girl I can take shopping and dress up," I said which made her laugh.

We got up and finally met the doctor at the front desk. She led us to the back room again with a smile on her face.

The nerves in my stomach were going crazy.

"Well, I am happy to say that you are having a...."

Chapter 15

After we left the doctor's office we went and grabbed something to eat and headed over to Erica's apartment. I wanted to tell Erica what I was having.

I was super happy to find out what I was having today and so was Laura. I was eating my food while she was driving, I fed her some of my food since she couldn't eat and drive at the same time.

Each time we stopped at a stoplight she would lean over and kiss me, and each time I would try to deepen the kiss, but a car would blow the horn.

By the time I finish my food we had pulled up to Erica's apartment. I cleaned myself up and cleaned the mess I had made. You would have thought a kid had eaten in here the way I made a mess.

"You fed my car more than you did yourself." I heard Laura say while laughing causing me to pout.

Once she saw me pouting, she stops laughing and kissed my lips. Her kisses always make me feel better.

After the kiss, I smiled at her and passed her the bag with the food in it that I kept in my lap the whole time.

We got out of the car and walked toward the apartment. I had my key still, so I didn't wait for her to answer the door this time.

I walked in to find them laying on the couch cuddled up looking at a movie.

Do they do anything else other than sit around this apartment and watch damn movies all day?

I laid across them making them both laugh.

"Well, hello to you too," Erica said while still looking at the T.V.

"I missed you both and I just came back from my doctor's appointment."

That got both of their attention causing them to sit up to fast making me almost hit the floor. Thanks to Erica's fast reflex she caught me before I could hit the floor, but I still gave them one of my glares.

"We didn't mean to sit up that fast." I rolled my eyes and got up and walked over to Laura who stops eating her food when she saw I almost hit the floor.

I sat in her lap but left her enough room to still eat her food.

"You okay love?" She asked me.

I nodded my head and glared back over at Erica and Erin.

"Stop giving us that look, it's scary and I said sorry," Erica said.

I sigh and lay my head back on Laura's shoulder.

"You could tell them now," Laura said.

Remembering what we had come over here for I sat up and my smile came back as if it had never left.

"What is there you need to tell us?" Erica said while getting up off the couch.

"We found out what I'll be having and I'm so excited!"

"Well, don't keep us waiting," Erin spoke this time.

That would be mean if I just got up and left without telling them what I was having, but I don't want to be mean right now.

"It's a girl!" I screamed out while getting up from Laura's lap.

They both got up and hugged me and Erica was just as excited as I was because we both love to shop, and we get to start our shopping.

We sat down and started talking about different names and none of them came to me, or I just wasn't feeling them. I'm not sure what I wanted to name my child, but I wasn't in a rush to come up with anything.

I looked at Laura a few times and wanted to know what she thought of the names they were coming up with, but she liked them all or she just wanted to get past this as much as I.

After another hour of different names, I was starting to get hungry and wanted to go out to eat.

They wanted to order something, but I didn't want anything to order, so I made them get up and get dressed to go out.

While they were getting dressed, I sat and talked with Laura.

"Would you want to be a mom?" I asked the random question that's been running through my head all day.

"I always wanted to be a mom, but I can't have kids." I started feeling sad when she said that.

Most women feel less of a woman if they can't have kids because that's what we are made for, to have kids.

"Would you be my daughter's other mom?" I asked her with hope going through my body.

I could see the surprised look on her face, but it didn't last long, and the biggest and brightest smile came across her face.

She got up from her spot and pulled me to my feet hugging me tightly. Once I was in her arms, I melted into her. Being in her arms made me feel safe.

"I would love to be her mom."

I looked up at her and smiled leaning in to kiss her lips. Kissing her lips felt like kissing a cloud they were so soft, and I could kiss her lips all day long. She pulled me closer deepen the kiss and a moan slipped past my lips.

We heard someone clear their throat causing us to pull away and turn toward the person.

Looking to see Erica and Erin standing there. Erica with her mouth open and Erin with a smirk on her face. This just got a little weird.

"Well, damn. I knew a professor and student dating would be hot but that was just wow." Erica said.

I laughed when Erin popped her upside the head for her comment because I wanted to do it myself.

"Okay, we're leaving in two different cars. We are going to my favorite place which you should know Erica." I said while pulling Laura toward the door.

I didn't wait to see what they had to say as I rushed her to the car. I don't know what has gotten into me, but I just wanted to get into the car where I can kiss her again without having someone watching us.

Once we got into the car, I pulled her face toward me and smashed my lips into hers kissing her hard.

What seems like 5 minutes was only seconds before we pulled away. I started kissing her neck and making sure to leave a mark behind.

A moan came from her, and it turned me on even more. I felt her nails dig into my hip I guess trying to control herself.

Pulling away from her neck I kissed her lips one more time and pulled down the mirror to show her my work.

"You didn't?" She said with shock written all over her face.

I nodded my head and sat back in my seat putting my seat belt on.

"I have work baby; I can't be going to work with this on me."

"Your mine and I need everyone to know that you are mine and mine only."

With that said she smiled at me and started the car pulling off from the apartment.

After having lunch with Erica and Erin, I went back to the house with Laura. I was still horny and needed to fix it fast.

When we got back to the house, I let her take her shower first and I went in when she came out.

I took an hour's shower making sure to shave the girl. There was a point where I started rubbing my clit and couldn't stop until a knock was at the door.

I finish taking my shower and got out dried my body off and got dressed.

Walking out of the bathroom to her sitting up in bed reading a book. I walked over to her and removed the book from her hands and got on the bed sitting on her lap.

"What has gotten into you today?"

I kissed her neck before answering her, "you look so damn sexy, and I been very horny all day." I said while moving her hand under my oversize shirt letting her feel how wet I am.

I wasn't wearing anything, but this shirt and it still felt like it was too many clothes.

She started rubbing on my clit causing me to bite down on my lip. This was feeling amazing, and I wanted more.

Pulling me toward her she started kissing my lips and I kissed her back trying to control the moans that were slipping past my lips into her mouth.

I bit on her bottom lip when I felt her fingers go inside me.

"You sure about this." I was only able to nod my head.

A few seconds later I was being pushed on my back and she was climbing on top of me kissing my lips slowly and soft taking her time with every move she made.

She went from my lips to my neck, and I moved my head giving her enough room to do as she, please. Feeling her sucking and biting on my neck cause me to get even wetter if that was possible.

I wrapped my legs around her pulling her into me more, I can feel the mark she was leaving on my neck.

Once she was happy with the mark, she left she pulled the oversize shirt off and started sucking on my breast that felt sore but amazing at the same time with her sucking on them.

I arched my back off the bed when she started sucking on them harder. Placing my hand on her head I pulled on her hair.

After she was done sucking on my nipples, she started kissing down my stomach and stopping at the top of my clit looking up at me.

I nodded my head giving her the okay to go further. She kissed my clit, and I took in a deep breath.

Not much longer did I have to wait before she started sucking on my clit and pushing one of her fingers inside of me.

My moans started soft, but I guess she wanted more, I felt another finger go inside me causing me to moan louder.

Her tongue played with my clit and found spots I didn't know I had there. She pushed her fingers in deeper and harder. I was no longer moaning but screaming.

"Fuck!" I moaned out.

I pulled on her hair making her face go deeper into my pussy.

"Oh gosh, don't stop." I was getting closer to my climax, and I think she knew it too.

She took her fingers from inside me in I felt her tongue take its place, and she started fucking me with her tongue.

"Oh fuck, I'm coming." I moaned.

Her grip on my hips tightens and not long after I was coming over her tongue and a deep long moan came from me.

Kissing my clit one more time before coming up and kissing my lips letting me taste my cum.

I kissed her back and sucked my juice off her tongue.

"You taste even better than I imagined you would." She whispered against my lips.

Laying on the side of me she pulled me into her, and I snuggled up closer to her laying my head on her chest.

Chapter 16

I woke up an hour early before it was time to get up and get ready for school. I looked over to see that Laura was still sleeping on her back.

Doing my best to not wake her yet I slipped under the covers and in between her legs. Happy that she doesn't sleep with anything on as well.

Last night I didn't get to please her because once she made me cum, I was ready to pass out and she didn't seem to mind.

Her legs were already open, so I lift her shirt some more. I had never done this before, but I was going to give it my best shot.

I rubbed my nose against her pussy taking in her scent but also being careful to not wake her.

Once my tongue slipped between her pussy lips, I fell in love with the taste of her. I started sucking on her clit slow and soft. She didn't make any movements or sound, so I kept going.

Removing the covers from over my head I looked up at her to see that she was still sleeping but soft moans were starting to come from her. Her hips started moving, I think she believes she is dreaming.

I sped up my pace and started sucking on her clit harder causing her to moan louder. I was loving the sound of her moaning and I wanted to hear more.

Pushing two fingers inside I started fucking her with them. Her hand went to my head and pushed my face more into her.

Feeling her getting tight around my fingers I knew she was getting close to her climax. I moved my fingers and started fucking her with my tongue trying to hit every spot that made her get closer to her climax.

Her body arched off the bed and her moan turned into a scream. I felt something splash against my mouth and I started drinking it knowing that it came from her. Her juice tasted like cherries, and it became my favorite kind of drink.

I licked up all her cum and climbed on top of her kissing her lips.

"Well, good morning beautiful." She whispered against my lips.

"Good morning momma," I said back to her causing her to smile big.

"We're doing this huh?" I nodded my head and kissed her one more time before getting off her and heading into the bathroom.

Not long after she was coming in behind me getting into the shower with me.

We didn't do anything in there but wash each other and kiss here and there. I could grow to love these types of mornings with Laura.

After we were done showering, she turned the water off and helped me out of the shower handing me a towel.

I dried off and walked out of the bathroom going into her closet since I didn't bring any more clothes over here.

"You really should bring more clothes over." I heard Laura say from behind me.

"I know I should, but then I wouldn't be able to wear your things and I love the smell of you on me," I whispered before kissing her lips.

I grabbed her sweatpants, tank top, and hoodie. I didn't need to worry about underwear since I made sure to bring lots of them.

Always remember if you don't bring enough clothes make sure to bring more underwear.

I got dressed and brushed my hair up into a messy bun. I looked in the mirror to Laura getting ready herself and her shirt is halfway buttoned because she was trying to rush and put on her shoes.

I walked over to her and started buttoning up her shirt for her. I grabbed the jacket to her suit off the bed. She looked amazing in this outfit.

Helping her put on her jacket I grabbed her work bag and passed it to her.

"No, time for breakfast I'm running late for class." She said while kissing me.

"I'll bring something for you so don't stop for nothing," I yell to her.

I still have an hour or so before it's time for me to leave for school. She had to leave early because she is a professor.

Knowing that I'm going to need to grab something for Erica too, I grabbed my things and locked up the house with the key she gave me.

Getting inside the car I started it up and let it warm up a bit. I haven't driven it since I been here because I make her drive everywhere.

I left the house and headed toward the school trying to see what I was going to pass on the way there. Remembering that I was going to ride past IHOP I started heading that way.

I got there in no time and got out of the car. I hurried inside and place my order, I made sure to get them both a coffee and me some orange juice.

Looking at the time I notice that I am doing great with time. She should have everything set up in class and Erica should be there as well when I get there giving them enough time to eat their food before the other students started showing up.

I paid for the food and left out after thanking the lady who passed me the food and drinks. It was going to be a little hard trying to get everything out of the car, but I was going to worry about that when I got there.

Thanking God that the school is right up the street and I have less than a 5minute drive.

125

When I got to the school, I thought I was going to have to search for a parking spot, but I lucked up and got one close to the door. I turned off the car and started grabbing my things.

I put my bag on my back making sure to put my phone in there. I grabbed the food and the drinks and locked up my car.

Someone was coming out of the building, and I yelled to them asking if they could hold the door. Happy the person was nice and stopped to hold the door as I asked, some people would have just looked and kept walking.

I thanked her and headed up to Professor Smith's class.

This is going to drive her crazy because she hates when I call her that, but I love it because it does something to her.

We're in school and I need to call her Professor Smith.

I walked into her class to her and Erica sitting there talking. I didn't care what they were talking about I just wanted to start eating before students started coming in.

They both got up when they notice me come into the room and started grabbing things from me.

"Why didn't you call me to help?" Erica asked.

I shrugged my shoulder and sat down and started eating.

"I wanted to hurry and get inside and sitting down there waiting for you would have taken too long and I'm hungry," I said with a mouth full of food.

Laura leaned over and wiped something off my face, and I smiled up at her.

While she was eating, I stole her coffee and was about to take a sip when it was taken from me.

I looked at the person who took the cup out of my hand, I notice that it was Mia. She is in both classes with me, and Erica and we are starting to become friends.

She knows that I am pregnant and that I am dating our professor.

"What was that for?" I asked her with a glare.

"Well, I saw you take it from Professor Smith when she wasn't looking, so I knew it was coffee and I know you can't have coffee. You're welcome." She said like it was that simple.

I rolled my eyes and looked back at Laura as Mia passed her the cup back.

The glare she gave me scared me a little, she hates when I try to drink coffee.

"Okay, I won't do it again just stop with the evil glare," I whined.

We finished our food right when the other students started coming in. Erica cleaned up the mess and I went and took my seat

We had a test today and I was told mine was going to be harder than everyone else, but I didn't care because I knew everything.

She passed out the test and everyone got to work. I looked at my test and almost died a little. She was right this was going to be hard.

Going through the questions I notice some of them were questions about things she hadn't taught us yet, but lucky me I read everything that we needed for this class.

I finish the test and go back over it again to make sure I was sure about my answers. I got up and walked over to her desk passing her my test.

"Done already." She asked me with a smirk.

I nodded my head and watched her check each answer. I thought I fucked up on this test but from the look on her face, I must have done okay.

"How did you even pass this like that?" She asked.

"I always read everything I need to know for a class even when the Professor hadn't taught it yet."

"Okay, you're free to leave or stay." I nodded my head and went back to my seat.

I pulled my phone out and started playing a game while I waited for Erica to finish her test, which didn't take long.

When she turned hers in, we grabbed our bags and left out the classroom with me blowing a kiss to Professor Smith.

"Fuck that test was hard," Erica said like the drama queen she is.

"Your test was easy, I had shit we haven't even learned about yet."

We walked down to the Café since it was not time for our next class yet.

Once we got to the Café, I order myself something to eat. I think I'm going to get fat while being pregnant because I eat almost every hour.

"How did you know everything on that test if she didn't teach it yet?" Erica asked me.

"I told you already, I read everything ahead of time putting me ahead of everyone else in the class."

We sat down at one of the tables and I started eating the sandwich I got, which wasn't what I wanted but I am too lazy to go out and get something to eat, and our next class starting soon.

"How are things with you and the Professor?" I looked up at her because that was a random question.

"Things are amazing, she wants to be a part of my daughter's life. Well, she would be her other mom." I said with a mouth full.

She had a shocked look on her face, and I couldn't help but laugh. I guess I'll be shocked too if my best friend told me something like that.

"Do she mean it?" I nodded my head and got back to eating.

By the time I was done eating it was time for our next class. We weren't doing anything in these classes but taking a test. That's only because it's getting close for us to finishing school, which is in another month.

I threw my things away and followed behind Erica. I looked over and saw she was smiling like a mad man.

"What's up with the creepy smile?" I asked.

"Erin is just being her sweet self. Every day she sends me these cute little messages letting me know how much she loves me." I smiled at that idea, but I wasn't in love yet.

We walked the rest of the way in silence. Once we got to the class we walked in and headed straight to our seats.

I just wanted to get these test's over and done with, so I can go home. I want to cuddle up and watch a movie with Laura.

Our professor passed out our math test, and we begin working on it. I looked down at it and saw I knew everything that was on there.

I skip the questions that I was going to have to show work and went to the ones that had multiple choice answers.

Going back to the ones I skipped I worked out the problems and looked back over my work before getting up and handing it in.

"You're free to go." The Professor said.

I grabbed my bag and lean over to Erica letting her know that I was going to go stop by Laura's class since this is her free period.

I left out the room making sure to close the door behind me and not letting it slam shut.

Walking down the hall I spoke to some people, and they spoke back. I must be in a good mood because I normally just stay to myself and let them walk right past.

I made it to her classroom and saw that the door was half-open, but I was able to hear voices.

Fighting against myself if I should just walk in or leave letting her have her privacy.

When I went to walk away the voice stop and my curiosity got the best of me. I pulled the door open only to find her and some other woman's lips locked together.

I was frozen in place. I couldn't move. I didn't know what I was supposed to do, so I did the only thing that came to me, I slammed the door and took off running out of the building.

I hurried and opened my car door and jumped inside before I closed the door, I heard someone calling my name, but I didn't care. I closed the door and started the car up pulling off from the school.

Chapter 17

All of them kept calling my phone and I wouldn't answer any one of them. Erica called to see where I was and to make sure I was okay.

Erin called because she was worried just like Erica was.

Laura called the most and left voicemails that I just delete. I didn't want to be around anyone.

I wanted to be alone and cry to myself. I gave myself to her and she goes around making out with other people.

I trusted her with parts of me I couldn't trust anyone with.

I even wanted her to be a part of my kid's life, well I still do, and I know she still does as well but that doesn't mean we have to be together.

She can be my daughter's momma and we could co-parent. Yea, that sounds like the best idea to go by.

Sitting on the grass with my ice cream in my hand I looked at the sky seeing the sunset. The different colors were amazing and I'm sad I couldn't see this with someone special.

Once I started eating my ice cream my phone started ringing again. I looked at it to see it was Laura calling again, I guess she doesn't get the hint that I don't want to talk to her.

I took in a deep breath and answered the call.

"Hello?"

I didn't say anything yet, I didn't know what to say honestly.

"Yeah?" I replied drily.

"We need to talk; I need to explain." She begged me.

Honestly, I did want to see her, but I wasn't sure if that was a good idea.

"Okay, explain then."

"The person you saw in my class was my ex-wife, she was begging for me to give her another chance and I told her no, that I was happy with someone else. I was telling her to leave but she kissed me I pushed her away, but you were already gone before I can explain anything to you." I listen to her, and I wanted to believe her but something in me just couldn't.

"I don't know Laura, it looked different from the way I saw it."

"I swear it wasn't, I don't want her. I need you I can't be without you baby. Please come back home." She begged.

My heart started beating fast when she called her house my home as well. I fought against the smile that was trying to come across my lips.

"Seeing that hurt me, Laura."

"I know, and I'm sorry. You're the only one for me, London." She sniffed.

My heart broke at the thought of her crying.

"Please don't leave me for something I didn't want to happen. I can't be without you." She begged again.

I thought for a while. Did I want to leave her? Of course not, she's the first person I grew feelings for.

"I'm not going anywhere; I'll be there in an hour or so."

I hung up the phone and went back to eating my ice cream. Once I was done with my ice cream I got up and went to my car.

Starting it up I headed straight to her house not wanting to waste another second being away from her.

I got to her house in 15 minutes since I was only at the park that wasn't far from her place.

I turned off the car and sat there for a few minutes trying to get my head together before seeing her.

Once I was okay, I got out of the car and walked up to her door using my key to get in.

The lights were on and the T.V. in the living room was going. I walked into the living room to see she was laying on the couch sleeping.

You could still see the tears that she cried when she was talking to me. I hate that I am the reason that she cried.

I softly wiped the tears that were starting to fall in her sleep. I guess she felt my touch and moved her face closer to my hand before opening her eyes.

The ocean blue eyes I'm used to seeing happy had nothing but sadness in them and that's something I never want to see.

"I'm sorry." She whispered while pulling me into her.

I nodded my head and held her closer to me. "It's okay, I forgive you," I whispered back.

We sat there in each other arms not wanting to let go of each other until my stomach started growling.

"You haven't eaten." She asked me.

I shook my head no, "only ice cream."

She pulled away and got off the couch pulling me with her into the kitchen.

"You need to feed the baby and yourself."

I sat at the table watching her make something quick. Honestly, I wasn't hungry, but I knew she was right.

Feeding the baby is something I'll always have to do even when I'm not hungry.

After we both ate, we went upstairs and took our showers and got into bed.

I snuggled closer to her holding on to her like if I don't, she would slip away somehow.

If I don't have her in my future, then there is no future because she is not in it. She holds the key to my heart, and I can't see myself without her.

I finally understand why I feel this way about her because I am in love with her.

My eyes started getting heavy and I knew I would be asleep soon.

"I love you." Was the last thing that was out of my mouth before I closed   my   eyes.

Chapter 18

I snuggled closer to the warm body that was next to me, I was comfortable and didn't want to wake up.

Not long after light kisses were being placed on my face making me giggle.

"Wake up sunshine," I heard her beautiful voice say.

I looked up and kissed her lips letting out a soft sigh against them.

"I don't feel good."

She rubbed my stomach, and I closed my eyes enjoying the feeling of her touch.

"Our little one giving you trouble huh?" I nodded my head and pouted my lips.

She didn't take long to kiss the pout off my lips and for me to melt into her. I kissed her back trying to deepen the kiss when the second alarm went off.

"Okay, I'm up let's go shower," I said while grabbing her hand and leading her toward the bathroom.

It wasn't time for me to get up, but Laura wanted me to ride to school with her. I think she wanted me to be stuck at the school until it was time for her to get off.

I'm okay with that because after my tests I can go into her office and sleep.

We took our shower together just enjoying our morning together, spending every morning with her makes each day feel better and brighter.

After we washed each other, we got out and start getting ready for the day. Today I went with some skinny jeans that are a little bit tighter than I can remember. I grabbed a black t-shirt and some sneakers.

Since I was done before her, I went downstairs and put on some water to make her a cup of coffee. I learned that her day never fully start until she had her first cup of coffee.

By the time I was done making her coffee she was coming down and heading toward the kitchen.

"Mm, that coffee smell good." She said while reaching for the cup.

I pulled it away from her and earned a glare from her. "Got to pay for it first," I said through my giggles.

She laughed herself and walked closer to me pulling me closer to her and kissing my lips softly. The way she kissed me made every breath in my body leave.

"Can I have that coffee now?" I was only able to nod my head and pass it to her.

She winked at me before taking the first sip of her coffee. I reach back for it because I wanted a sip, and I don't think one sip can hurt the baby.

Before I was able to take the cup from her hands, she had already moved it out of my reach causing me to pout even more. Between her and Erica they will make sure I don't eat or drink anything I'm not supposed to.

"Baby just one sip," I begged.

She took a minute before she answered me, I guess taking some time thinking it over. Once she made up her mind, she passed me her cup and I smiled at her.

I took a sip making sure not to drink too much and upset her.

"Thanks, my love," I said before kissing her lips.

She smiled against my lips, and I pulled away to look into her eyes. Looking into her eyes is like looking into the ocean and you just never want to look away.

"I love you," I whispered.

Her eyes lit up at the sound of me telling her I love her.

"I love hearing you say those words. I love you more." I smiled and looked over at the stove for the time.

139

"It's time for us to leave out or you're going to be late for work."

She gave me another kiss before grabbing her things and I followed behind her going into the living room to grab my bag for school.

Once the house was locked up, we got into the car and pulled off from the house.

Since I took my test for her class already, I don't have her in the morning anymore, and since Professor Williams wanted to be an ass and give us two different tests making us come in for his class.

I can't wait to finish school and walk across the stage. I know I don't have any family to be there for me, but I do know that I have my best friend Erica, I have my lover Laura, Erin, and my new friend Mia.

I was busy in my head that I didn't know we had pulled into the school until Laura snapped her fingers in front of my face pulling me out of my head.

"What's got you zoning out?"

"Just thinking about how happy I am to have you all in my life and how I wouldn't change that for the world." I smiled at her and got out of the car.

We grabbed our things from the back of the car and headed inside the building I'll soon be saying goodbye to.

Before leaving the house, I text Erica and let her know that I won't be at the Café this morning and that she can find me in Laura's class.

I thought she would have come to school around the same time we normally come, but when we reached Laura's class she was sitting outside the door on her phone.

If it wasn't for Laura clearing her throat we would have been still standing here wondering when she would notice us.

She looked up at us and stood up before putting her phone away. "You didn't have to come this early you know," I said.

"Yeah, I know but I wanted to, and I miss my best friend." She whined.

I laughed and hugged her, "you just saw me yesterday at the house."

"I know but I got used to you being at home and now I have to get used to coming over to Professor Smith's house." She giggled at the end.

I looked over to Laura whose face was turning red. I smiled at her and she gave me one back before opening the classroom.

"Well, tomorrow I have another doctor's appointment, would you come with us?" I asked.

"I'll love to." She jumped with excitement.

We helped Laura get her class together before it was time for us to head to class ourselves.

We left out of Laura's classroom and headed to Professor Williams's class to take our last test for the year.

I didn't get why they were making us take our test a month before we graduate, but I didn't care because we wouldn't have to come back to school until graduation day.

It didn't take me long to finish my tests because I knew everything, they were going to ask us on the test.

Staying up all those nights and learning everything I can were paying off and I'm glad I did because I can just run through my tests and leave this damn building, so I could sleep for however long I want.

After I was free to go, I walked to Laura's class, since I knew she had a class going I text her and told her to come out into the hallway because I didn't want to disturb her class.

I waited for her to come out into the hallway and when she did, I smiled big at the sight of her.

"How did the test go?" she asked me while pulling me into her arms.

"It went great, I'm pretty sure I passed every one of them with a high A," I said before kissing her lips.

"I'm proud of you, my love." She said once she pulled away from the kiss.

Hearing that made me feel joy inside my heart and I wanted to hear it again because I never heard someone say they were proud of me.

I looked back up at her and noticed the worried look on her face. I went to ask her what was wrong until she wiped the tears I didn't know were falling.

"What's wrong?" She asked me in a soft voice.

"I just never heard someone say they were proud of me," I tell her the truth not seeing a reason to lie.

She kissed my cheeks where she wiped the tears from and pulled back looking into my eyes.

"Well, now you will hear it so much that you might get tired of hearing it." She laughed at the end.

I giggled and kissed her again. "Can I lay in your office until you get off? I'm tired."

She nodded her head and pulled me into her class causing her students to look up at us. Some spoke, and others were busy with their test.

She gave me the key to her office and walked me back out of the room. I kissed her lips again and pulled away heading toward her office. I turned around and told her that I'll leave the door unlocked.

Once I got into her office, I took my shoes off and lay across the couch that was sitting in the corner of her office.

As soon as my head laid down sleep took over my body and I was out within seconds.

I don't know how long I was sleeping but I felt someone shaking me. I open my eyes to come face to face with my lover smiling down at me.

"Feeling any better." She asked me, and I shook my head no causing her to have a worried look on her face.

"When was the last time you ate?" She asked randomly.

I thought about it and come to realize I haven't eaten since yesterday evening, and it was a whole new day.

"Yesterday?" I said more like a question.

"Come on get up we're going to get something to eat and if that doesn't work, we're going to see the doctor."

I nodded my head and sat up with her help. I put my shoes back on and grabbed my bag which she had just taken from me and told me to lock up the office.

I did as I was told and locked up the office and followed her out of the building and toward her car.

"What do you want to eat?" She asked me while pulling out of the parking lot.

"I'm craving burgers."

She looked over at me and nodded her head. There was nothing, but silence left between us and I started dozing off again because she was massaging my scalp with her free hand.

She shook me lightly to wake me up again and I looked around to see where we were at. It was some fast-food place that I haven't been to before.

"Where are we?"

"This is Milly's Burgers; they have the best burgers in town."

We both got out of the car and headed inside. When you walked through the door, you are hit with the smell of burgers and everything else they cook.

My mouth started watering for the burgers that smelled stronger than anything else.

We walked up to the counter and waited for someone to come to take our order. I looked over to Laura who seems to know what she wanted already.

"What are you getting?" I asked.

"The burger combo." I heard the word burger in it, so I just went with what she was getting.

"I'll take that too, order for me I have to use the restroom," I say before leaving to go to the bathroom.

I used the bathroom and washed my hands before leaving out of the bathroom. I looked for Laura to see that she had found a table for us.

I walked over to her and set down in front of her.

"While we're waiting why don't we come up with some baby names?" I asked.

When Erica and Erin were coming up with baby names, I didn't want to use them because I wanted me and Laura to come up with something together.

We both started thinking about names and none was coming to my head for a while until one popped in.

"What about Sophia?" I asked

"I like Sophia but more for a middle name. What about Emma Sophia?" She asked with a smile on her face.

Emma Sophia, I said out loud, liking the sound of it.

"I love it."

"Me too, where did Sophia come from?" She asked.

"It's Erica's middle name, so don't tell her until the baby is here and is already name. I want to surprise her with it."

We talked some more before the food came and it looked amazing. The burger was a nice size, and I knew I was going to eat it all by the way my stomach started growling making me turn red and Laura start laughing.

We started eating in silence. I started with the burger while Laura ate her fries first. I didn't want the fries, but I ate some here and there.

Once I got done eating, I was feeling a lot better, I guess I just forgot to eat being worried about taking them damn tests.

She leaned over and wiped my mouth and I thanked her before drinking the lemonade that she ordered for me. She knew me well because I don't drink anything but lemonade when I go out to eat.

"Feeling better now?" I nodded my head and took the other part of her burger that she stopped eating.

I giggled when she gave me a look that said how the hell can you still eat.

"Don't judge me I'm eating for 2 okay," I said with a mouth full.

I finished eating the burger and something came to me, I wanted my daughter to have the last name of my lover, but I didn't know how she would feel about that.

"What do you think of Emma Sophia Wilson-Smith?" I asked hoping she wouldn't freak out.

Her eyes popped open, and I thought I had killed my girlfriend for a minute because she didn't say anything or blink.

I snapped my fingers in front of her face and called her name snapping her out of it.

"You want to give her my last name?"

I nodded my head, "Yeah, you're her mother as well and she should have both her mother's last name."

She smiled and leaned over the table kissing my lips and pulling my bottom lip between her teeth sucking on it causing me to let out a soft moan.

"I'll love it if she takes on my last name." She whispered.

Chapter 19

It's now time for my third appointment this month, I hate that I need to go twice a month.

I'm only two months pregnant and I'm not sure why I have to keep going twice a month. Laura said that it's to make sure the baby is growing healthy.

I just went along with it and got dressed for my appointment. I think I am just in a mood today and I don't know why.

She was dressed before me and left me in the room to finish getting ready. I just threw on a dress and some ankle boots and pulled my hair up in a messy bun.

I walked downstairs to see her at the stove cooking and from the looks of it she was making pancakes that I can't seem to stop eating.

I sat at the table and waited for her to finish. Normally I would kiss her this morning, but I am just not in the mood right now.

She placed the pancakes in front of me with syrup all over them the way I like it. I wasted no time and started eating.

Once I was done, she was looking at me with a smile on her face. "Feeling better now?" She asked.

I nodded my head and smiled back at her. "Thanks love." I stood up and washed my dish out and walked over to her and kissed her lips.

"Finally, I get my morning kiss I've been waiting for." She says dramatically.

"I'm sorry, I don't know why I was cranky this morning," I tell her while hugging her close to my body.

"It's fine my love, I know you're going to have your mood swings and I'm still going to be right by your side." She said before kissing my nose making me giggle.

I looked at the time and sigh, it's getting closer for us to leave and get this over with.

She helped me grab my bag and I locked the house before getting into the car. I text Erica and made sure she was still coming, and she told me she was.

I'm glad the traffic wasn't bad because we got to my doctor's office in 20 minutes. After she parked, I grabbed my bag I keep all my things inside that I needed for the doctor.

Looking around the parking lot I didn't see Erica's car and I was hoping she would be here before us.

Laura walked around the car and grabbed my hand giving me a smile that I couldn't help but smile back. I followed her lead and walked toward the building that I'm starting to think of as my third home.

When we walked inside Erica was sitting there with Erin and some girl on the side of them. I walked over to them and set on Erica's lap.

"Finally, you're here we've been waiting for an hour." She said dramatically.

"She's lying we just got here 10 minutes ago," Erin said while laughing.

"Well, there goes my guilt trip into getting free dinner." Erica mumbles.

I shook my head and hugged her before getting up from her lap and hugging Erin next.

I felt someone staring at me and I knew it wasn't Laura because she was sitting on the other side of Erica on her phone.

Turning toward the girl who was sitting with them when we walked in. She was the one staring at me and I was starting to feel uncomfortable under her stare.

I waved at her and went and sat in Laura's lap making her put her phone down to hold me in her arms.

"Oh um, this is Emily," Erica said sounding like she didn't know what to say.

"Hi, I'm London and this is my girlfriend, Laura."

She waved at me, but she didn't stop staring at me and I wanted to call her out on it, but I didn't want to come off as being rude.

I forgot I needed to sign in and got up from Laura's lap and walked over to the front desk.

"Appointment for London Wilson," I tell the lady sitting behind the desk.

Once she had me signed in, I went back to my spot in Laura's lap. She must have felt that I was getting uncomfortable and turned to the girl that was still sitting with us.

"What's wrong?" She whispered in my ear.

I turned my body to where my head was in the crook of her neck. "That girl keeps staring and it's making me uncomfortable," I whispered back.

She turned her head and saw that she was still staring this way.

"Ask her about it." I shook my head no.

She looked at me then back to the girl Emily. "She looks a little like you." She whispered causing me to snap my head up and stare at her.

Before I can say anything, my name was being called to see the doctor. I got up and grabbed Laura's hand and waited for them to get up as well.

Erica leaned over and whispered something in Erin's ear causing her to nod her head. When she got up and Erin didn't, I guess she told her to stay here with that Emily girl.

We walked to the person who called my name and went into the room where the doctor will do my check-up.

As always everything is fine, and my baby is healthy and so am I. Erica was upset that she still couldn't hear the heartbeat-like she wanted to, but Laura got to see the baby like she wanted to, and I just wanted to get the hell out of here.

Being happy that I was free to go I got dressed and dragged them both out of the room heading back into the waiting room where Erin and Emily were still sitting.

"How did everything go?" Erin asked.

"It went great, the baby is healthy, and this one is cranky," Erica said while walking over to her girlfriend, so I wouldn't hit her.

"Why don't we all go back to my house?" Laura asked.

I looked at her and back at everyone and gave a small nod before walking out the door with them following behind me.

Someone caught up to me walking on the side of me and I look to see that it was Erin.

"Who is that girl? And why does she keep staring at me?" I asked her since she and Erica seem to know her.

"Honestly, I don't know she showed up at the apartment and talked with Erica while I took my shower. When I came back out Erica said she was coming with us to your appointment." I nodded my head letting her know I understand.

I got to Laura's car and waited for her while she was talking with Erica who kept looking over here at me.

Once she was done talking, she came over and opened the door for me before going to her side of the car and getting in herself.

I wanted to ask what they talked about but if they wanted me to know they would have told me.

I let the seat down and closed my eyes to take a nap until we reach the house.

Laura placed her hand on my thigh and started rubbing it while she was driving, I guess she knows I sleep best when she is touching me.

I knew we were home when I felt the car stop and Laura stop massaging my thigh. I wanted to stay asleep, but I knew I needed to get inside the house since we are having guests.

With my eyes, half-closed I got out of the car and waited for Laura to get the rest of her things while I just left mine in the back seat of the car.

When she was done, I followed her to the door and leaned on her while she was unlocking the door.

Right, when we walked into the house there was a horn behind us, we both turned around to see Erica's car pulling into the driveway. I left and went into the living room leaving Laura there at the door.

Once I laid down on the couch it didn't take me long to find sleep. I don't know why I was so tired, but I just couldn't stay awake.

I felt my head being lifted and someone sitting down and placing my head into their lap. When the fingers started running through my scalp, I knew it was my lover.

When I heard Erica come in loud, I knew I wasn't going to be able to stay asleep for long.

Laura

I knew that when she went into the living room that she was going to go lay down and try to sleep some more.

I should have asked her doctor about always being tired like this. I know when you get pregnant that you do get tired and want to sleep because your body is changing to fit a human inside it, but she sleeps all day when she doesn't have school or work.

Leaving the door open for them I walk into the living room and saw her sleeping in her favorite spot on the couch. I took the spot I normally sit at which is next to her head with her head in my lap and me massaging her scalp.

I learned that when I do this she sleeps more peacefully.

Not long after Erica came in loud, and I knew London was going to be up once again and might be even more cranky.

I shush her and point at my love letting her know she is sleeping, which I know she needs to be up because this Emily girl needs to talk to her about something.

Erica was trying to tell me who she was, but London wasn't standing that far from us. She told me to just make sure London doesn't freak out and have a panic attack.

I got nervous about what was going to happen because if she thinks that London was going to have a panic attack it had to be something bad.

Leaning down I whispered into her ear, "Beautiful, I need you to get up."

She mumbles something but sat up and leaned against my shoulder with her eyes still closed.

I shook my head and started kissing her neck which I know is sensitive and would cause her to moan out. She jumped awake and looked at me like I lost my mind, and I couldn't help but laugh.

London

When she started kissing my neck I jumped and glared at her. She laughed and tried to pull me into her, but I pushed her away.

"Come on baby, I'm sorry." She whined trying to make me give in.

156

One look into her eyes and I was going to. I can never stay mad at her. I went into her arms and allowed her to hold me close.

"Who wants to order the food?" Erin took out her phone and started looking up places to order from.

"Pizza?" She asked everyone.

They said yes to the pizza, "I want wings." I told her, not being in the mood for pizza.

She placed our order online which will be here in half an hour. We sat around the living room talking, well everyone but Emily.

I stopped the conversation and looked at her because she was doing that damn staring again.

"I want you to stop doing that. It makes me very uncomfortable when you stare like that. Do you know me or something?" I asked in an angry tone.

"I um." She seemed lost for words like she couldn't find her voice.

Erica leaned over to her and whispered something in her ear, and she nodded to it.

"I'm Emily Ava Brown and I think you're my sister."

Chapter 20

I don't know if I stop breathing or if the room just froze in place, but it was one of them I'm just not sure which one.

Nothing was coming into my mind, no words, no thoughts, no sound. Everything was just blanked.

I snapped back in when someone forced me to look at them when their face stops being blurry, I saw it was Laura.

"Follow my breathing." She told me.

I didn't know what she was telling me until I notice that my breathing was getting heavy, and I was breathing very hard.

Doing as she said and followed her breathing until mine even out.

Everyone in the room had a worried look on their faces and I can understand why. I don't know why I started panicking I just did.

"Okay, I'm fine now," I said with a small smile before getting up and leaving out of the living room.

Going into the kitchen to grab a bottle of water, I stood there drinking the water and staring into space until the water was gone.

I went back into the living room and asked Emily to follow me. When she got up, I went upstairs, and she followed behind me.

I went into one of the guest rooms not wanting to take her into our room. I open the door and let her in first and closed the door behind me.

We both got comfortable on the bed neither one of us saying anything.

After another moment of silence, I took it upon myself to break it.

"What makes you think I am your sister?" That was the first thing that came out of my mouth.

"You look just like my daughter but an older version of her." She replied pulling something out of her purse.

She passed it to me, and I looked at it, and it was a picture of a little girl that looks just like my baby pictures.

"She's beautiful," I whispered.

"Thanks, that's my little Abigail." She said over my shoulder.

I passed her back the picture and looked at her better than I did when I first met her. Looking at her now, I can see that we do look a little alike.

"Why didn't you say anything when we first met at the doctor's office?" I questioned.

"I was going to, but Erica said to wait until after your appointment was over."

There is just one thing I am not understanding about this how did she know where to find me or who my friends were?

"How did you find me?"

"Honestly, I just learned about you 5 years ago and I have been looking for you ever since because I wanted to meet the person who is supposed to be my baby sister." She said with teary eyes.

She took in a deep breath before talking again, "my father finally told me after my mother passed that I had a sister out in the world somewhere, but he didn't know where she was or how to find her. That he cheated on my mom after they fought."

I looked at her and back down at the floor. She had to learn that her father cheated on her mom after her mom passed away. Mother was just a one-night stand, but she didn't care though because she and my father fought a lot.

"He said he gave the woman his number after and told her to call him sometime, but she didn't call until 3 months later telling him that she was pregnant, and she didn't want him a part of the child's life."

I listen to her tell me how she found out about me and everything that her father told her that had gone on during that time.

"Once I found out that I had a sister I started looking any and everywhere. I didn't have a name and I didn't have a picture of her, the only thing I had was the name of the woman who was supposed to be her mom."

I looked at her and saw that the tears she was trying to hold back had started falling.

"I started to give up when I couldn't find that woman anywhere until about a week ago. My neighbor told me that it's a girl who goes to school with her that looks like an older version of my daughter. I begged for the name and what school she went to; she gave me everything I needed."

I grabbed the tissue off the nightstand and passed her one getting a small thank you in return.

"So, the other day I went to the school early hoping to see this girl who looks like my daughter and that's when I noticed you walking into the building with Erica, at that time I didn't know her name. I stayed out there until your class was over with, I was going to come up to you, but I got scared and well just followed Erica to where she stayed and talked with her."

I should be feeling creeped out right now but for some reason, I don't. It's like part of me is glad she went through all of this to find me.

"She told me about your appointment today and I asked if I could come along, and she said yes to just come to her apartment and we will leave together and that's what I did. I didn't mean to stare at you the way I been doing but I was amazed that you were there and that you could be my baby sister."

I'm sure she thinks I might not be listening to her because I haven't said a word yet, but that's only because I want to hear everything.

"The only way for us to be sure that I am the person you are looking for is to take a blood test," I tell her, and she nodded her head.

"That's fine with me."

"You said I'm your baby sister, how old are you?"

"I'm 28, which means I was 5 when you were born. I know your 23 because I asked Erica about you."

I nodded my head back at her letting her know I understand.

"I'm sorry I dropped this on you like this, but I just needed to meet you. I always wanted a sister and I had one, but I just never got to me her. How was your life growing up?"

I wasn't sure if I could trust her but something in me told me that I could trust her with my life if I had to.

"My life was good growing up until I turned 13," I whispered loud enough for her to hear.

"What do you mean until you turned 13?" She questioned.

"Once I turned 13 the man, I thought was my father started raping me at that age and my mother let him. I didn't get away until I was 17 but he ended up finding me again a few months ago."

I looked up at her and saw tears forming in her eyes again.

"I thought I was safe from him when I left but I was wrong, he found me and raped me again but this time giving me the little girl that's growing inside me," I said while rubbing my belly.

"I thought we were going to have the same father until I had to go into the police station and talked with the officer that was on the case and found out they had my mom. I went and talked with her, and she ends up telling me that he wasn't my father and that's why she allowed him to do whatever he wanted to me." I said with a cracked voice.

"After he was done, I snapped back into reality and remember I put knives all around my apartment because I was scared to be alone and that he would find me. I noticed the knife under the table that we were by, and I grabbed it and stabbed him with it. He bled out on my floor."

I felt her arms wrap around me and a part of me felt whole like it knew it was missing something. I turned around in her arms and held onto her tight.

"I'm so sorry I wasn't there to protect you." She whispered in my ear; it was like she already knew the answer to the blood test.

"I'm sorry I couldn't be there for you." She whispered over again. I felt tears hitting my shoulder and I knew mine was hitting hers as well.

"It's okay now, you didn't know about me, and I didn't know about you," I reassured her.

We sat like that for I don't know how long, we only pulled away when my stomach started growling making us both giggle.

"I'll talk with my doctor about doing a test tomorrow," I tell her while wiping my face and her doing the same.

"Okay, little sister now let's get some food into that stomach of yours before it growls at us again." She said while giggling.

We got up and left the room heading downstairs where I started smelling the food. I don't know how long we have been up there, but it must have been for a while.

I walked over to Laura who was eating some pizza and sat on her lap hugging her tight. It was like I just needed her touch right now.

"You're okay love?" She asked me.

I leaned up and looked into her eyes and they turned into worry I guess seeing that I have been crying. "I'm okay now," I said with a smile and kissed her lips earning a whistle from everyone else.

I hid my face in the crook of her neck to hide the blush that was creeping onto my cheeks.

Emily sat on the other side of Laura making me have no choice but to stay in her lap because I needed to be closer to her.

Erica passed me my food and I wasted no time eating. I was hungry and wanted to eat anything in my reach.

We sat and talked while we ate, everyone asking Emily questions about herself.

"When the test comes back, and it says that we are sisters, can I meet your daughter that same day?" I asked.

"Sure, I would like that." She said with a big smile.

The one thing I haven't asked her is about the man that's supposed to be my father. I'm not sure if I wanted to know anything about him, or if I ever wanted to meet him but I knew I needed to know something about him.

"What's your father's name?" I asked.

"Logan, he's an amazing father and a great grandfather. You would love him." She said with a smile on her face.

I knew she had an amazing childhood growing up and I felt a little jealous because mine wasn't great, but I wouldn't change it for the world. If my life didn't go how, it did, I wouldn't have met Erica and I wouldn't have fallen in love with Laura.

I smiled at her and nodded my head not knowing what else to say. The only thing I was hoping was true, is that she was my sister, and I finally had a sibling, an older sister at that and I would be an aunt and so would she.

Chapter 21

Last night I didn't sleep because I had a lot on my mind and everything that Emily told me wouldn't stop playing in my head.

I'm sure I kept Laura up last night as well because I was tossing and turning all night long.

I didn't go to sleep until she pulled me into her arms and laid my head on her chest. I don't know why I didn't do that in the first place, but like I said I had a lot on my mind, and I wasn't thinking.

Right now, I am still in bed in the afternoon with Laura's head in my lap close to my stomach while she reads a story to the baby.

She didn't go to work today because she wanted to go with me to do the blood test this morning. I told her she didn't have to miss work for this, but she wasn't taking no for an answer.

Honestly, I'm happy she stayed home today because I didn't want to be alone, and I wanted to spend some time with her.

I let out a sigh and pulled the book from her hands making her look up at me.

"What is it, love?"

"I need to start looking for an apartment and get back to work."

When I told her that she sat up and faced me. "I don't want you to leave." She said sadly.

"I don't want to leave either but we both know I need a place before the baby comes."

"You can stay with me, it's like you live here anyway. We can pick one of the guest rooms to turn into her room." She begged me.

I smiled at the idea of staying with her and becoming a real family. I always wonder what a real family would be like.

"Okay, I'll love to move in with you," I said with a big smile on my face.

She pulled me into her and kissed my lips hard causing me to moan. I kissed her back before pulling away.

"Now let's go pick out a room for her and then we can get dressed and head out to the stores." She said while pulling me off the bed.

We walked out of the room which is the master bedroom and went to our left to the second biggest room in the house.

"Would this be too big for her?" She questioned.

"Nope, because I want to get a lot of stuff, and I'm sure Erica and Erin are getting a lot of things as well. Emily said she would get some things too."

"They do love you, but I love you more." She teased.

"I love you as well, now it's shopping time, and let's not forget to call Erica to meet us."

We went and got ready to leave the house and I called my best friend and Emily to meet us at the mall.

I knew they all wanted to be a part of this, and I wasn't going to leave them out on anything.

Once I was dressed in my sundress and my hair was pulled into a messy bun, I grabbed my shoes and put them on before heading downstairs toward the kitchen.

The first thing I saw was grapes I grabbed them and washed some off to take out the house with me, making sure I grabbed enough for the both of us.

It didn't take us long to have the house locked up and get into the car. Making sure I had everything before she pulled out from in front of the house. Once I was sure I gave her the okay to leave.

I was eating the grapes and looking out the window watching the world pass by. I took one grape and placed it in front of her lips. She opened her mouth and took the grape while running her tongue across my fingers and sucking on them.

I was frozen by this action and the lower part of my body felt like it was set on fire. That turned me on and so many ways. I can feel how wet I have gotten, and I knew if I didn't do anything about this before we got to the mall, I was going to be cranky from being horny.

Grabbing her free hand without thinking much about it and placing it under my dress letting her feel how wet she had made me by that little action of hers.

She looked at me with a shocked face at how wet I was.

Her hand found its way into my panties, and she begins to rub slowly on my clit. I opened my legs more and laid my head back against the seat closing my eyes.

Her eyes were on the road, but it was like her mind was focusing on making me climax.

Two fingers were pushed inside me, and I bit down on my lip trying to hold in my moan because we are in the car and I'm sure people can hear outside this car.

"Don't hold it in baby let me hear you." She whispered while moving her fingers faster inside me.

Her fingers started hitting my spot and I couldn't help but moan. She removed her fingers from inside me and went back to rubbing on my clit fast and hard. I was getting close to my climax.

"Fuck, don't stop baby I'm almost there." I moaned out.

Taking that as a hint she sped up her pace and my legs started shaking, a few seconds later I was moaning louder and coming all over her fingers.

"Fuck!" That was all I was able to say.

She pushed her fingers inside me one last time before pulling her hand out of my panties. I watched her as she sucked my juice off her fingers one by one. Fuck, that was sexy.

By the time she stopped licking her fingers, she was parking the car in the mall's parking lot.

When she put the car in park, I pulled her face toward me and kissed her lips, sucking on her bottom lip. She pushed her tongue inside my mouth, and I sucked on it tasting myself on her tongue.

We finally pulled away in need of oxygen, if I was able to hold my breath for a long time, I would still be kissing those soft ass lips right now.

"I need to go to the bathroom before we meet up with everyone," I tell her once I got air back into my lungs.

We got out of the car and headed into the mall going straight for the bathroom. I need to use it and clean myself up.

After we were done in the bathroom, I called everyone to see where they were and lucky, they were all together waiting on us.

We walked out of the bathroom holding hands and heading toward the kid's area of the mall.

We finally found them in one of the stores looking at different outfits. They were all so cute and I just wanted to buy them all.

Honestly, I just wanted to focus on getting small things for the baby. Like onesies, blankets, and a baby bed. You know all the good stuff.

We walked up to them, and I hugged everyone.

"Thanks for coming," I tell them.

A little girl ran past me and up to Emily, I knew this was her daughter because she looks like a mini-me.

"I had to bring her because she didn't want to stay with her mama." She tells me.

This whole time I thought she was with a man but turns out she is with a woman.

"It's okay." I smiled at her before bending down to the little girl.

"Hi, little one."

She waved and hugged onto her mommy's leg. I can't wait to meet my daughter and know the feeling of being a mom.

Emily bent down as well removing Abigail from her leg, "remember when mommy told you that she might have a sister?" She asked her, and Abigail nodded her head.

"Well, this is her. This is London." She said while looking at me with a sparkle in her eye.

Abigail looked up at me and back at her mom before a big smile came across her face and she hugged me taking me by surprise.

Once that was over, we started shopping.

I grabbed some of everything and so did Laura and everyone else. I even grabbed something for Abigail. Emily told me not to, but I was going to do it anyway because she wanted it and she could be my niece.

By the time we made it to our 5th store, I got hungry, and Abigail got cranky.

"Let's go to the food court and get something to eat." They all agreed, and we started walking toward the food court.

In the middle of walking Abigail was tapping on my leg, I looked down to see what she wanted. She lifted her arms wanting me to pick her up.

"Abigail she can't walk with you," Emily tells her, but I pick her up anyways.

I didn't see anything wrong with picking her up since my belly is not showing and she is very light.

Once I had her on my hip, I started back walking with Laura by my side keeping an eye on me with every step I made.

We made it to the food court, and I wanted pizza. "What do you want to eat sweetie?" I asked the little girl in my arms.

"Pizza." Her cute little voice said.

"Great choice because I want pizza too."

My lovely girlfriend goes and orders the pizza for me, her, and Abigail since everyone else wanted something different.

I sat at the table with Abigail and let everyone else leave to go get the food. Emily wouldn't leave until I had to make her because she thought it was a problem to leave Abigail on me.

I played with her and allowed her to play with my phone while we waited for the food. She did things on my phone I didn't know I was able to do. Kids nowadays know a lot.

When I noticed Laura coming back, I sat Abigail in her seat on the side of me and left the other side for Laura to sit next to me putting me in the middle of the two.

I helped her set everything down and stole a kiss in the middle of it. "I love you."

"I love you more my love." She said with a smile.

There is no way I'll get tired of hearing her say that.

We sat down and started eating without waiting for everyone. I helped Abigail with her food making sure she didn't make a mess.

"You seem happier than normal."

"Well, I am, thanks to you."

When she asked me to move in with her that made my day and put me in the best mood, but when she made me cum in the car that put me over the moon.

"I'm glad I had part of that." She spoke.

We went back to eating and by the time we were almost done the others came walking toward us.

I laughed when they saw we had already eaten.

"How the hell did you eat that fast?" Erica asked.

"Well, I was hungry, and I didn't want to wait for you all to come back from that long ass line you were in," I said.

They sat down and started eating. We talked while they ate, and they wanted to know if I came up with a name for the baby, I told them I have but they can't know yet.

They started talking with each other while Laura and I had a conversation about what we were going to do to the room.

Lucky the guest room we picked didn't have anything in there but a bed and a dresser. I didn't want to move all that stuff out of the bedroom.

"We should do the walls light pink with white." She spoke.

"I like that and think she would as well."

Chapter 22

It's been about two weeks now and I got a call from the doctor who did the blood test letting me know that the test is back, and we can come in today.

I called Emily and let her know what the doctor said. She going to meet me there with her wife and daughter.

I couldn't shake the nervousness I was feeling right now as Laura drove closer to the doctor's office. I kept playing with my fingers, something I did when I got nervous.

Laura grabbed my hand with her free hand and held it in her hand trying to calm me. It worked a little, but I was still a little nervous.

"Everything is going to be fine love." She tells me.

I believe her, but I just feel like I will be hurt if it didn't come back that she was my sister. We spent the last two weeks together getting to know each other. Her daughter is so damn sweet, and my heart will break if that little girl wasn't my niece.

Feeling the car stop I looked up to see that she had just parked the car in the parking lot.

"You ready to find out if you have a sister?" She asked.

I nodded my head and got out of the car waiting for her to lock the car up. Once she was by my side, I grabbed her hand and we walked toward the building.

We walked in and saw Emily and her family sitting in the waiting room.

As we were walking up to them Abigail saw me and jumped from her mommy's lap and ran over to me. I couldn't help but laugh when she hugged onto my leg.

I bent down and picked her up kissing her cheek.

"Hey, little one," I said while walking toward Emily.

"Hey, Emily."

"Hey London, this is my wife, Madison." She said while grabbing her wife's hand.

"Hello, nice to meet you," I said.

"It's nice to finally meet you as well." She said with a big smile that can light up the whole room.

"Have the doctor come out yet?" I asked Em.

"Yes, but we were waiting for you."

I nodded my head and went up to the front desk with Abigail in my arms.

"Hello, we're here to see Dr. White," I tell the lady behind the desk.

"Right, she told me to bring you straight to the back when you got here."

I waved my hand to them telling them to come on. I couldn't wait to get this over with, so my nerves could get a break.

We followed the assistant to the back where she took us to one of the empty rooms to wait for the doctor.

It was not long before the doctor came in with an envelope in her hands and a smile on her face.

"Alright, glad everyone is here now." She said while taking her seat.

I passed Abigail to her mommy and sat in Laura's lap. I watched as she took the paper out of the envelope and read them to herself.

It was as if the time had stopped, and everything was stuck in place. The seconds were moving slowly.

"Well, the test has confirmed that you both are sisters." She said with a big smile.

I was happy that the test came back how I wanted but it didn't stop me from being shocked.

I was brought back to reality when someone pulled me into a hug and held me tight. I knew it was Emily and I hugged her back just as tight.

"Finally, I have got you in my life." She whispered.

Feeling something wet hit my shoulder I pulled away and looked into her eyes to see tears of happiness and I'm sure they were in mine as well.

Wiping her tears away I hugged her again. "Thanks for looking for me and never giving up."

She pulled away and walked over to her wife and grabbed her daughter and walked back over to me.

"Now she can finally say she has an aunt." She said while laughing.

"Yeah, and I can say this little one is my niece."

I looked up to see Madison walking over to us, "Welcome to the family, sister-in-law." I giggled at that.

This is another amazing thing that happened in my life. I walked over to Laura and hugged her.

"I have a sister."

She wiped my tears and kissed my cheeks. "I'm happy for you, my love."

We went out to eat to celebrate, we invited Erica and Erin to join us which they didn't waste any time saying yes to.

We all made it to the restaurant at about the same time. Being that it's close to Erica and close to the doctor's office we were at.

All of us walked in at the same time and Laura spoke to the waiter to get a table for 7. 1 kid and 6 adults. It didn't seem like it was a lot of us, but I guess it is.

We took our seats and order our drinks before looking at the menu.

I was in the mood for steak, so I went with the steak dinner. Once I knew what I wanted I placed my menu down and waited for the waiter to come back and take our orders.

"What are you getting?" Laura asked.

"I'm going with the steak dinner."

"I'll go with shrimp pasta," she said.

Once everyone knew what they were getting we called the waiter over and placed our order.

After the orders were placed, I got up and went to the restroom. I felt like I haven't been to the bathroom all day, but I know I have.

By the time I came back from the bathroom some of them already had their plates. I guess I was in the bathroom longer than I thought.

I took my seat back by Laura and laid my head on her shoulder. She kissed the top of my head and pulled me into her.

"Everything okay love." I nodded my head and yawned.

"Just tired," I said through another yawn.

5 minutes later our food came. It smelt amazing and I just wanted to dive right in. When the plate was placed in front of me, I thanked the waiter and started eating.

Eating this steak felt like I have died and gone to heaven, that's how amazing it was.

I didn't think I was going to finish that big steak, but I did and now I feel fat because I want something sweet now. I guess I'll wait till we head home and have her stop at the store.

I leaned over to her and whispered in her ear, "on the way home can we stop at the store for ice cream?" I asked.

"Of course, we can love." She said while giggling making them look at us.

I felt my face heating up from them staring and I just wanted to run away, but the only thing I was able to do was to place my face in the crook of her neck.

"Lo, now that we know we are sisters would you like to meet our father?" I heard Emily say causing me to sit up straight.

I thought about this for the last two weeks, if the test comes back saying that she is my sister would I want to meet the man who didn't have a chance to meet me as a baby.

181

I couldn't come up with an answer, or a thought. I didn't know the answer to the question she asked me.

It felt like I couldn't breathe. My breathing felt uneven, and the room looked like it was starting to spend.

"Baby, look at me. Follow my breathing, listen to my voice." I heard a voice say and tried to do as it said.

It wasn't working, and my vision was getting blurry. I tried to find Laura in the middle of this blurriness, but it wasn't working either and everything started going black.

Chapter 23

I heard a beeping sound like a machine going and felt someone holding my hand. What the hell happen? The last thing I remember was being out to eat with everyone and Emily asked me something.

Whoever was holding my hand I squeezed it letting them know that I was up, and they can let go now but that didn't happen.

"Oh, God! You're up." I heard the voice of the one who owns my heart.

I open my eyes and look at her and smiled.

"What happened? Where am I?" I asked her while looking around.

"We're at the hospital, you scared everyone." She spoke.

I was able to hear the sadness behind the words and I didn't mean to scare anyone. I don't even know how I ended up here.

"I'll go get the doctor." She kissed my cheek before leaving out the room and returning a few minutes later with my doctor behind her.

"I'm glad that you're up Ms. Wilson." The doctor said.

"Me too, why am I here?"

"You had a bad panic attack causing you to blackout which is not good because you are pregnant, but the baby is fine."

I'm glad she said that because I was about to panic again thinking that I hurt my child.

I couldn't help but feel sad still because there was a chance that I could have hurt her, or even worst lost her for good.

When the doctor left the tears finally start falling and I curled myself up in a ball on the bed.

Laura climbs into the bed with me and held me as tight as she could.

"It's okay my love." She whispered to me.

"I could have hurt her, and I don't know why I panic." I sob.

"Shh, you didn't hurt her and that's all that matters. You panic when Emily asked you if you wanted to meet your father." She tells me.

Right, I do remember that. "I didn't mean to panic; I didn't think she would ask me that right away."

She wiped my tears and kissed my cheeks. "It's okay, you might have had a flashback of the man who you thought was your father. I'm sure your real father will do anything to protect you." She tells me before kissing my lips.

I kissed her back and placed my head on her chest. It didn't take that long for me to fall asleep in her arms.

Laura

I knew she was going to go to sleep once she placed her head on my chest, that seems to be the only way she goes to sleep.

I reached for my phone in my back pocket to text Erica and let her know that everything was okay and that the doctor wanted to keep her overnight to monitor the baby and her.

I'm glad they put her in a big bed because there is no way she is letting me go with how tight she is holding on to me.

I love this girl and it's only been a few months since we were dating, and I'll already do anything for her.

Love knows no time; it comes when it wants to and I'm glad it came when I met her.

I pulled the thin hospital blanket over us and kissed her head before going to sleep myself.

I woke up when I heard the room door close and looked up to see the doctor coming in. I tried to sit up without waking her, but she started moving around, then settle back down after a while and went back to sleep.

"Just coming to let you know you're free to take her home. Everything is fine, make sure she takes it easy with the rest of the pregnancy." She tells me.

I thanked her and grabbed the papers from her hand and watched her leave out of the room. I started kissing all over London's face trying to wake her which took a good 5 minutes.

"Come on love, let's go home and get you into bed."

When she heard that she could go home she sat up fast. "Slow down love," I said while laughing.

She smiled at me and kissed my lips. I helped her get dressed and we left the hospital heading home.

Once we got home, we went straight up to the room and had a quick shower and got into bed.

She found her way to her favorite spot on my chest. "I was scared when she told me I blacked out from a panic attack. I could have lost Emma." She whispered against my chest.

"Well, you didn't love and that just means she wants to be here just as bad as we want her here. I can already tell she's a fighter." I said while rubbing her belly.

I turned on the T.V. and played a movie for us to watch until we fell asleep.

London

186

I wanted to stay asleep, but something was missing keeping me from staying asleep. I opened my eyes to see that Laura was out of bed.

I stretched out my body before getting out of bed and going into the bathroom to do my morning routine.

Once I was done, I walked out of the room calling her name trying to find where she was at.

"Down here love." I heard her yell.

I followed her voice downstairs in the kitchen at the stove making something to eat. I walked up to her and hugged her from the back missing her touch.

"Couldn't stay asleep huh?"

"No, you weren't there," I whispered.

"Well, we slept all day and I know you needed to eat something, so I came downstairs and started cooking dinner."

I kissed her cheek and went into the living room and lay across the couch turning on the T.V. looking for some type of crime show to watch.

I was lost in the show that I didn't hear Laura calling my name until she paused the show.

"I was watching that," I whined.

"I know, but I need you to eat."

Getting off the couch I followed behind her and headed into the kitchen. Whatever she made smells amazing, and I can't wait to try it.

I didn't know I was this hungry until my stomach started growling.

We sat at the table to eat and talked about everything. She's going to have someone come out and paint the room the colors we want.

I told her we could do it ourselves, but she doesn't want me around the paint, and I understand why.

Once we were done eating, we went back up to our room to watch movies in bed and just relax for the day. Since the weekend is almost over, she goes back to work.

We watched some romance movie, but I wasn't paying attention to it because I was tired and just wanted to be held which she didn't have a problem with.

I cuddled closer to her and soon was on my way to sleep.

Chapter 24

It's been two weeks since I had that panic attack and blacked out. Laura makes sure to call me every chance she gets to make sure I am okay and don't need anything.

Emily blames herself for my panic attack, but I keep telling her it's not her fault, I just need to get comfortable with knowing that my real father isn't anything like the man who raised me.

Right now, I am sitting in the waiting room of my doctor's office because it's that time of the month for my check-up. I drove myself this time because everyone was busy and didn't have the time to bring me.

Laura wanted to come but I didn't want her to miss any more work. I'll just have to start making my appointments over the weekend that way she could be here for them all.

I heard my name being called and I got up from my seat and walked over to the nurse who would take me to the back.

Once I got inside the room, I put on the gown they always make me put on for some odd reason.

By the time I had the gown on my doctor was coming through the door.

"Good morning Ms. Wilson." She said with a cheery voice.

"Good morning, Dr. White," I said with a smile.

I laid on the bed and let her do the check-up waiting for her to finish this up, so I can go home and stuff my face with ice cream.

"Well, everything is great as always. Your blood pressure is still doing good, not worrying me like the first appointment. Now, let's check on your baby girl."

I nodded my head and prepared myself for this cold gel to hit my stomach, but I could never prepare myself for it because it still gives me chills.

I watched the screen as she rubbed the gel on my stomach looking for the baby. It didn't take long for her to pop up on the screen, still little as ever.

I can't wait to see what it would look like when it gets close for her to be here.

I still have a few more months before I'm able to hear her heartbeat and I can't wait.

"Everything is still fine, nothing to worry about, but I do want you to take it easy to try to avoid anything that might cause you to have a panic attack." I nodded my head letting her know I understand.

"I'm not sure if I told you to because it's not written down in your file, but I want you to start taking prenatal pills during the pregnancy. You can get them from any pharmacy."

"Okay, I'll grab some on the way home."

We finish my appointment up and I was free to go and make my next one. I got dressed and left out the room heading toward the front desk.

"I need to make my next appointment," I tell the lady sitting behind the desk.

I don't bother to learn their names because it's always a different person when I come to my appointments.

"What day would you like to have your next appointment?" She asked.

"Do you have any weekend appointments?"

She typed on the computer, and I waited a few seconds until she started talking again. "We can put you in for Saturday at 9:30 AM."

"That would be perfect."

I'm glad they are open on Saturdays because I want Laura here every step of the way.

"Okay, you're all set for your next appointment in two weeks." She said with a smile.

"Thank you and have a nice day," I said before walking away and heading out of the building.

I got into the car and headed to the closest pharmacy to pick up some prenatal pills. Connecting my phone to the car I call Laura.

"Hey, my love how did the appointment go?" Her voice came through the car making me smile.

"It went amazing, I wish you could have come with me."

"I do as well, but we both know I don't need to miss any more days at work."

"Yeah, I know but the next one you will be able to go to I got it on the weekend."

We talked while I drove to the store, I told her about the doctor wanting me on prenatal. Of course, she wanted me on them too but forgot to ask my doctor about them.

"I'll see you when you get home from work. I love you."

"I love you more." She said before hanging up the phone.

I parked the car and went inside the store trying to hurry and get these pills. I went straight to them and picked the one I believe is best for me and went up to the counter to pay for them and some snacks I grabbed along the way.

Once I got home, I took a shower, made something to eat, and took one of the prenatal pills.

After I was done, I cleaned my mess and went upstairs and lay in bed watching T.V. hoping that it put me to sleep.

I felt arms wrap around me and kisses being placed over my face causing me to smile.

"Wake up love." Her voice sang through my ears.

I kept my eyes closed and pulled her closer to me snuggling into her.

She started kissing down my neck before sucking on it causing me to let out a soft moan. That was like a sign to her because she started sucking on my neck harder, I'm sure leaving a mark behind.

I opened my eyes and pulled her lips toward mine and kissed her hard and deep. She slid her tongue inside my mouth, and I wasted no time sucking on it.

She started taking off the little clothes I had on, and I was taking off hers as well. I wanted her body against mine and these clothes weren't leaving fast enough.

Once all clothes were off, I slid down a little and popped her nipple into my mouth. Sucking on it and running circles around it with my tongue while using my free hand to play with the other one.

I gave the same attention to the other nipple making them both hard. She was trying to keep her balance above me while I was working on her breast.

I finish sucking on her nipples and slid down some more leaving kisses down her stomach.

Once I got to her pussy, I placed kisses over it before pulling her clit into my mouth. I moaned from the taste of her and started making circles around her clit with my tongue.

I grabbed onto her hips making her stay in place as she sits on my face. Slipping my tongue inside her making her moan out louder.

I started moving her hips making her grind on my tongue as I move it around inside her.

Making my way back to her clit, I started sucking on it harder and faster.

"Fuck!" She moaned out.

Finding her spot on her clit with my tongue I started sucking on that one spot, wanting her to cum all over my face and in my mouth. I wanted to taste every part of her.

"God, right there." She moaned louder.

I didn't have any plans of stopping any time soon.

"Fuck, this is going to be a big one baby."

I didn't care how big she came, I just wanted it all over my face and mouth.

Seconds later she let out the biggest moan I heard from her followed by her juice squirting all over me.

I sucked and drank all of her and kissed it once she rode out her orgasm.

She slid her body down my body and started kissing my lips, sucking on my tongue tasting herself.

"Mm, I taste even better when on your tongue." She moaned softly.

She started rubbing on my clit causing me to moan.

I knew it wasn't going to take me that long to climax because I was turned on to the max and needed a release badly.

We spent the rest of the day making love and cuddling with each other. The best way to end a day.

Chapter 25

Graduation day:

It's the day of graduation and I'm nervous because I invited my sister and her family. I even told her to bring our father because it was time for me to meet him.

She kept asking me over was I sure about that because she didn't want me to panic again. I don't know what will happen when I meet him, but I know it's time that I do.

I was pulled out of my thought when I heard my name being called.

"London Wilson, graduating with honors and the top of all her classes." I heard my family cheering me on and my best friend pulled me into a hug before I walked on stage.

I shook all their hands and took pictures with them as well. When I got to Laura, she pulled me into a hug and hugged me tight, kissing my cheek.

Once I had my degree in my hand, I got off the stage and took my seat, and waited for everyone else name to be called.

I did the same to Erica when they called her name. I'm very proud of her like she is of me.

I'm glad that is over with because it was too long, and my ass was hurting sitting in that damn seat for too long.

I looked around for Emily and found her standing outside with everyone else waiting for their loved ones to come out.

Emily ran up to me and hugged me tight with a big smile on her face. "I'm so proud of you baby sis."

I blushed at her calling me baby sis, that's something I need to get used to hearing.

I felt small taps on my leg and looked down to see my little niece with flowers in her hand. I bent down, and she gave me the flowers before hugging me.

"Thank you, baby girl. They are beautiful, did you pick them out yourself." She nodded her head and took my graduation hat.

"Come on he's here." I heard Emily say.

Before I followed her, I looked around for Erica or Laura. I feel like I need either one of them with me.

I spotted Erica and waved her over and she came, I told her I was about to meet my father for the first time, and she understood what I needed.

She grabbed my hand and I squeezed it a little letting her know that I am nervous. We followed behind Emily and her wife as she led us to where he is.

It wasn't that much of a walk, but once we stopped, there stood a man who had the same green eyes as me and both of our hair is light brown.

It's like I was looking at a male version of myself. I looked at Emily and she only had green eyes like us, but her daughter had everything like me and this man.

Emily grabbed my hand causing me to let go of Erica's and pulled me closer to the man standing there waiting.

Once we got close, she hugged him. "Hey, daddy."

He spoke back with a deep voice. "Hey, baby girl."

"I'm no longer the baby no more, this is your daughter London Wilson." She said while pointing at me.

"Lo, this is our father, Logan Brown."

I smiled at him and waved not knowing what I'm supposed to do.

"It's finally nice to meet you my child, and congratulation on graduating from college."

I stepped closer to him and stared at him for a while before speaking. "Thank you, and it's good to meet you as well father," I said before hugging him.

I surprised myself and everyone else when I hugged him and didn't panic. He wrapped his arms around me, and I felt like I was safe from any and everything.

We pulled away with both of us having tears in our eyes.

I smiled at him and thanked him for coming. I didn't see Laura walking toward us until she was at my side.

"Congratulation my love, I'm so proud of you." She said while kissing my cheek.

She wiped the tears that were falling and looked up to see we were standing in front of my father.

"Love this is my father, Logan. Dad, this is my girlfriend, Laura."

They shook hands, "It's nice to meet you." Laura said, and he said the same thing.

We all went in our cars and met up at a restaurant. I was happy when Erica's parents showed up. I haven't seen them in so long. I hugged them both telling them I missed them.

"It's been so long, mama and papa," I said using the name I gave them for myself.

"I know child. You need to start coming by the house more." Mama said.

She was right I do need to start going by the house more, I miss her cooking and listening to papa screaming at the T.V. when his team is losing.

"I'll keep that in mind."

We all went into the restaurant and the waiter showed us to our seats. We had a big table since it was a lot of us.

Being around everyone made me feel very happy.

We didn't take long to place our order since everyone knew what they wanted and Laura being Laura she had to try something new.

"So, London how far along are you? Erica told me you are pregnant." Mama said.

I smiled at her, "I'm going on 4 months in a week."

"Do you know what you're having?" She asked.

"Yes, a girl."

"Well, I always wanted to be a grandma." She said with a big smile.

I smiled just as big because she is like a mother to me, and my baby girl will have one grandma and two grandfathers.

"What about names? Picked them out yet." Papa asked this time.

I nodded my head letting everyone know that we did pick out names.

Erica's eyes glared at me, and I tried my hardest to not look her way. She knew we picked out names but she's mad that we won't tell her what we picked.

"When are you due?" Emily's wife asked.

"On Erica's birthday. May 16."

"Wait, I didn't know you were due on my birthday."

"I know, I wanted to surprise you but now you know." I smiled.

We started talking about who was going to spoil my daughter more and who was going to have her more. It was funny watching Emily and Erica go back and forth.

Everyone stopped talking when our food came and started eating.

Once I finish eating, I got sleepy. This baby is going to make me fat before she even gets here. Sleeping and eating are all that I do now. I leaned my head on Laura's shoulder and closed my eyes trying to get a quick nap in.

I heard Madison say, "That's how you used to be when you were pregnant with Abigail." Everyone started laughing.

Laura kissed the top of my head and I snuggled closer to her. I didn't care if we were out to eat, laying on her always made me go to sleep faster.

"Come on love, let's get you home and into bed," Laura said while grabbing our things.

I don't even know who paid for dinner, but I didn't care I just wanted to go home and snuggle up to my lover and go to bed.

Chapter 26

6 months pregnant:

I'm now six months pregnant and I'm showing. My belly is big, meaning I might be having a big baby or that I am just fat now.

Every day when Laura gets off work, she makes me go walking because it's supposed to make giving birth easier.

She still makes sure I'm taking those damn pills every morning before she goes to work.

Right now, we are at my doctor's appointment and waiting to be called to the back. This is the day we are going to hear the baby's heartbeat and I can't wait.

I felt the baby moving and grabbed Laura's hand to let her feel. It's like Emma already knows who Laura is and moves whenever she hears Laura's voice.

"Oh wow, she's moving a lot in there huh."

"Yes, kicking the hell out of me."

Ever since I was able to feel the baby move, she did nothing but kick me, it got to the point where when she pushes any part of my body you were able to see the outline of it. It looked so weird but amazing at the same time.

We heard the nurse call my name and we went into the back to the room where the doctor will give me my 6th-month check-up.

"Good morning, ladies." Dr. White said while walking in.

"Good morning," Laura and I said at the same time.

"Let's get started with the check-up."

She did everything that she normally does, and everything is still how she wants them to be.

Now it's time for us to see the baby, that's the best part of the check-up if you ask me.

She placed the gel on my stomach, and I got chills like always, but it didn't last that long. I was starting to get used to it.

"Oh wow, this baby going to have a head full of hair when she gets here." The doctor said.

I looked at the screen and can see where her head is pointed down like she was ready to come already.

"Is she sucking her thumb?" Laura pointed out.

"That she is you have a thumb sucker on your hands." The doctor said while laughing making us laugh as well.

"Are you ready to hear the heartbeat for the first time?"

"Yes, we have been waiting for this day to come for a while now," I said.

After a few moments of silence, there was a heartbeat being heard and I couldn't help the tears that started falling.

"Oh gosh, that's the sound of our little one's heartbeat," I said to Laura.

"Yes, and it's the most beautiful sound I have ever heard."

"Everything is fine, she has pointed the right way because time is going to fly by with these next 3 months." I nodded my head as I listen to her.

"Are we doing a natural birth or pain medicine?" She asked us.

"I want to do natural," I tell the doctor but looking at Laura.

"Okay, natural it is. I wish you the best of luck mama." She tells Laura while laughing.

I looked up at Laura and saw her look worried and scared at the same time. I mean there is going to be some pain but I'm sure I can handle it.

"It's going to be fine, my love," I tell her while sitting up and kissing her cheek.

We finished up the appointment and headed out of the building going back to the house.

Today is the day that the stuff we order online will come and I don't want to miss it. I want to finish putting together the room.

It's already painted and looks amazing with the colors we picked.

"We need to go shopping for the house," Laura said as she opened the car door for me.

I nodded my head and told her we can go while we were out.

We went to the store closer to the house which I am thankful for. We grabbed everything that we were out of, and I grabbed more ice cream.

"How can you eat ice cream like that?"

I shrugged my shoulders, "I don't know but it's amazing." I said with a big smile on my face.

We finish our shopping and head to the counter to check out.

"Awe what a beautiful couple." The elderly woman said while checking us out.

"Thank you," Laura said.

As she was checking us out, I grabbed a candy bar and had her ring it up as well and pass it back to me.

Laura shook her head and giggled causing me to frown.

"What?" I asked.

"It's nothing my love, you can have as many candy bars as you want." She said before kissing my cheek.

I smiled at her and started eating the candy while she paid for the food.

I helped her put everything in the car and got into the car while she put the shopping cart away.

It didn't take long for us to get home and have everything put away. By the time we got home some of the things were already there and we had to drag them into the house.

The baby bed is what came first, once we had everything put away, we took the baby bed upstairs to the room and started putting it together.

I didn't think it would be hard putting a baby bed together, but it was hard, and it took us a while before we had the damn thing together.

Once we had it put together, I left the room and went downstairs, and grabbed some ice cream.

By the time I took my first bite, Laura was walking into the kitchen with a smile on her face. She walked up to me and kissed my lips.

"It's getting closer for her to be here, and we almost have everything together." She said with a big smile.

I know she is just as excited as I am for the baby to come.

"I can't wait to finally meet her. It feels like I been pregnant forever."

She rubs on my belly and smiles at me, "you don't have that much longer to go."

I nodded my head and fed her some of my ice creams. As we were in the middle of eating ice cream there was a knock at the door.

"I'll get it," Laura said while walking toward the door.

I stayed in the kitchen feeding my face with ice cream.

I heard her answer the door and things went quiet until she came back into the kitchen with my sister.

"Hey, baby sis." She said while walking up to me.

"Hey, big sis," I said with a smile.

"How are you feeling?"

"Fat and hungry."

Every day Laura tells me I'm beautiful and that I'm carrying our baby, so I'm not fat. Which causes me to smile every day.

"You're not fat my love, you're beautiful with a glow." My lover's voice rings in my ears.

I smiled up at her and asked her to cook me something to eat, I am craving pancakes, but she doesn't mind cooking them.

"Okay, the baby going to come out asking for pancakes because that's all you eat." She said while laughing.

I stuck my tongue out at her and gave her a smile at the end.

My sister and I sat at the table and talked for a while. She was out shopping and wanted to stop by and see us. I wish she would have brought Abigail because I wanted to see her cute little self, but she left her with her momma.

"Oh, come see the baby room," I said while dragging her up the stairs.

Once we got to the room, I open the door, I let her walk in first.

The best part of this room is that we have Princess written over her bed but left some space to add her name once she was born.

I didn't want to put her name yet because I knew I would want to show them the room.

"Wow, this is beautiful I love the colors."

"We're still waiting for the changing bed to come, which is supposed to be tomorrow."

"You two putting this stuff together by yourself?"

I nodded my head, "well, more like she's putting it together. She doesn't let me do much."

We walked around the room and talked until Laura called me down to eat.

I walked her to the door and hugged her goodbye before going into the kitchen. I sat at the table where she had the pancakes waiting for me the way I like them.

"Thanks, babe," I said with a mouth full.

I can tell how much I have changed in the past 6 months. Everything I was afraid of doing I now do with no problem.

I used to tell myself I would never love because no one wants someone who is broken inside and out, but here I am with the love of my life.

Chapter 27

Who knew you would have to buy all kinds of clothes when you were pregnant? It's getting to that point where I can't fit anything, and I need to go shopping.

I haven't been working because Laura doesn't want me working right now, so I haven't applied for any teaching jobs, and everything I need or wants she gets for me.

I told her if she keeps spoiling me like this, I'll never want to get a job again, but we both knew that was a lie because I love working.

Since Laura is at work and can't take me shopping, I called up the next best person in my life.

Erica is on her way over here, so we can go shopping and spend some time together since she has been working, and I have been busy getting ready for the baby, so we haven't had any time together.

I grabbed the one dress that I was still able to fit for now and put it on. I let my hair stay in its curly mess and I grabbed my shades off the dresser.

I made sure I had my purse, phone, and the credit card Laura gave to me. By the time I went downstairs, there was a horn blowing outside. I looked out the door to see that it was Erica.

Locking up the house and walking to her car, well more like wobbling to her car. I got into the car and put my seat belt on and hugged her.

"I missed you."

"I missed you more." She said while rubbing my belly.

There was a time when I would get mad at someone rubbing on my belly, but I got past that now and didn't care anymore.

"Ready to head to the mall?"

I nodded my head and pulled my sunglasses down on my face.

We made it to the mall at a good time and didn't have to worry about NY traffic.

We lucked up and got the parking spot for pregnant women which I was glad about because I didn't want to walk too far.

Going into different stores and finding clothes that will fit me was not as hard as I thought it would be. I found all kinds of dresses, shirts, and pants that would fit me and still look good on me at the same time.

We went into a store for kids, and I found some things for the baby and my niece. I know my sister is going to be mad at me because I have two bags full of stuff for her.

After we were done shopping, we went and grabbed some Chinese food. We sat and talked, and she told me about the kids she was working with at her job.

She's a social worker, so she deals with kids all day long. She tries to help the parents out and make sure they have everything they need to get their babies back, but some don't care to have them back, so she tries to find a good home for them.

"Can we make a few stops before you take me back home?"

"Yeah, but first we need to get some gas, or we're going to be walking." She said making us both laugh.

We threw away our things and grabbed the bags and headed toward the car.

There were moments when I had to stop and take a breath because I couldn't breathe. It was a lot of work walking with this belly and all these bags, but I made it to the car.

We went to the gas station, and I filled her car up even when she told me not to but we both know I don't listen, and I do as I please.

"Where to first?" She asked as she got back in the car.

"First let's stop and get some food for me to take to Laura."

We went to Laura's favorite burger place and got her a burger combo. Honestly, I just wanted to see her but why not bring her some food while I'm at it.

I looked out the window as the outside passed by and different cars passed us by.

When the car park I noticed that we were at the school, and I was daydreaming out the window.

"Okay, I'll be right back because she has a class going on and I don't want to belong in there."

I grabbed the food and got out of the car heading into the building I once spent my days and nights in.

Someone held the door open for me as I was walking up and thanked them before going inside.

I went up to her classroom and knocked on the door getting her attention and some of her students as well.

I waited until she opened the door and allowed me into her class.

"Hi, my love." She said with a big smile.

I smiled back at her and kissed her cheek while handing her the food.

"I brought you lunch because I knew you didn't bring anything to work with you, plus I wanted to see you."

Her class went awe causing me to blush and I look down at the ground trying to hide it.

"I went shopping today and grabbed some clothes that will fit me better and some things for the baby. I also grabbed a few dresses I thought you would like to wear." I tell her as we walk back to her door.

"Thank you beautiful, I'm sure I'll love them." She said before kissing my lips.

"Be safe and don't work yourself too hard. I have a meeting today, but I'll be home right after." I nodded my head and kissed her one last time before leaving the building.

As I was leaving someone was coming in and I looked up just in time to see that it was Mia.

"Mia!" I said with surprise and happiness.

"Omg! London you look amazing, and the baby glow is working for you."

"Thank you, how are you doing?"

"I'm doing amazing, back in this damn school another 2 years."

We both laughed knowing that we hated going to school.

"Hey, did someone name Emily ever find you." She asked causing me to stare at her for a minute.

"Wait, you're the one who told Emily about me?" I asked her, and she nodded her head.

"Yes, we been neighbors for a few years and when I met you, you looked just like her daughter, but I wasn't sure, so I let it be until I finally told her. She almost broke her neck trying to turn toward me."

"Yes, she found me, and turns out I'm her sister," I tell her with a big smile.

We talked for a little bit more before saying goodbye to each other. I headed back to the car and told Erica what just happened and how Emily found me.

"Where to next?"

"Emily's place. I need to give Abigail her things."

We listened to the radio and song along while we waited at a red light. I missed these days with her, and I miss our girl's night.

We were singing in the car to Emily's house. Since it was a quiet area, I turned the radio down low.

She parked in the driveway where there was only one car there which was Madison's. Being happy that Emily is not home I got out of the car and grabbed the bags from the backseat.

Erica got out of the car as well and grabbed the bags from me as we walked up to the door.

I knocked on the door and we waited a few seconds before the door was pulled open.

"London, Erica what a wonderful surprise." She said with a smile.

I hugged her and walked inside the house calling for my niece. It didn't take me long to hear her little feet running toward the living room.

When she got into the living room, she ran up to me and hugged my leg. I bent down a little and picked her up sitting her on top of my stomach making both Erica and Madison freak out.

"It's fine she's not that heavy," I said while taking a seat.

"Auntie brings gifts for you as always."

Her face lit up and the biggest smile came across her face. I put her back down and told her to get the bags from Erica.

"You stay bringing her stuff, she going to be spoiled worse than what she is now." I heard from behind me.

I looked up to see that Emily just now coming home.

"Damn, I thought I was going to be able to sneak this time," I said while laughing.

"Mhm, she going to think she can have any and everything," Emily said.

"Well, she can because she's a princess. Isn't that right niece?" I asked her, and she nodded her head pulling out the clothes and toys I got.

"I was out shopping for myself and saw these outfits and just had to get them for her, they were too cute to leave at the store," I tell Emily.

We sat around and talked, and I made sure that they were going to be at the hospital with me when I had the baby.

Knowing that I have a wonderful family now makes me smile even more   each   day.

Chapter 28

I'm now seven months and I missed my doctor's appointment because I overslept, and I wouldn't get up.

Laura called and made me a new appointment which is in two weeks.

I was still lying in bed when Laura came back into the room with food and my pills. I wasn't hungry, but I knew I needed to try to eat something for the baby.

I sat up in the bed and she put the plate on my lap and the orange juice on the nightstand. I started eating here and there. Picking through the food.

Laura was watching me, and I could see that she was worried but I'm sure whatever it is, I'll get over it soon.

"What's wrong love?"

"I'm not feeling well." Once those words left my mouth, I was running to the bathroom hoping that I made it there in time.

I made it to the bathroom and the little breakfast I did eat didn't stay down. Laura was by my side in seconds making sure I was okay.

"I thought I was past this," I said with a small laugh.

She placed her hand on my forehead, "You're burning up." She said while helping me clean my face.

Once we were finished in the bathroom, she helped me back into the room and bed. She left and went back into the bathroom and came back out with a rag in her hand.

She climbed into bed and placed my head on her chest with the rag against my forehead. I let out a sigh and closed my eyes.

Not long after I was sleeping on her chest with a cool rag against my forehead.

When I woke up the second time, I was feeling a lot better. I don't know what happen, but I didn't like it and I hope it never happens again.

I sat up to find Laura sitting at her desk on the computer doing some work. I got out of bed and walked over to her and hugged her from behind.

"How are you feeling?"

"Much better but still a little tired."

"You gave me a scare there for a second, I end up calling your doctor while you were sleeping but she said if it goes away there shouldn't be anything to worry about." I nodded my head letting her know I understand.

I got back into bed and turned on the T.V. while she finished up her work. 30 minutes later she was joining me on the bed.

We snuggled together and watched Law and Order SVU.

On Monday I was feeling a lot better, and I was back to eating how I was, and Laura was getting ready for work.

I was eating breakfast while Laura was drinking her coffee and getting ready at the same time.

I may or may not have turned her alarm off, so she couldn't go to work today. I wanted to have her to myself today. I don't know why I was feeling more clingy than normal.

"I still can't believe you turned my alarm off and now I'm running late for work." She said causing me to frown.

I felt my eyes getting watery and I got up from the table and walked into the living room not saying anything to her.

My emotions were all over the place and I didn't know why or how to control them.

She walked into the living room and sat on the side of me, but I wouldn't look at her.

"I'm sorry, I didn't mean to yell." She said in a soft voice.

221

I turned to her and lay in her arms, and she wiped the tears away that were falling. Once I was calm, I lay on the couch, and she got up to leave the house for work.

"I love you and I'll be straight home after my last class is over with."

"I love you more," I yelled back.

I invited Madison over since she didn't have to work, and Abigail was at daycare today. I wanted to spend some time with her, since we don't talk much, and she is my sister-in-law

We were sitting in the living room watching a movie and talking about her and my sister.

"We met in high school, she was the nerd, and I was just me. I fell in love with her the moment I laid eyes on her." She said with a big smile.

I can tell it was true because she lights up whenever she talks about Emily.

"That's beautiful, love at first sight, I didn't think it was true."

She tells me more about how they started dating and everyone called them school goal coupled. Their high school year sound amazing, unlike mine.

In the middle of us talking I felt pain, but it wasn't as bad as the next one, I felt causing me to scream out in pain.

"What's wrong?!" She yells over my screaming.

"It hurts." I cried out.

She laid me back against the couch and checked me to see what was going on.

"Oh god no!" She yelled while running to grab her phone.

"Maddi, I don't feel too well." I cried out.

The pain was getting worse, and everything was starting to get blurry. I tried to sit up but fell back down on the couch.

"Don't move Lo, help is on the way." She tells me while wiping my face with a cool rag.

Before I knew it, I was starting to blackout and the sound of Madison's voice sounded far off.

Laura

I was sitting in class when my phone went off and it said that London was calling.

"Hello."

"Laura, this is Madison you need to meet us at the hospital fast."

I didn't know what was going on, but she sounded worried, I grabbed my things and turned to my students that were in my class.

223

"Okay, class is over with for the day I have to leave. I'll just pass everyone on this test since I need to go." I tell them while walking toward the door.

They hurried and grabbed their things and left out the door and I locked it up behind them.

I text one of the professors and told them to tell my other classes that the class is canceled today.

I jumped in my car and pulled out of the parking lot heading toward the hospital.

I'm sure I ran a few red lights and some stop signs, but I didn't care I needed to get to London and fast.

Making it to the hospital in 10 minutes when it's at least 30 minutes away from the school I knew I was speeding.

I parked my car and ran into the hospital and up to the front desk.

"I'm here for London Wilson," I tell the lady.

Before she can say anything else I heard my name being called and I turned around to see Erica coming up to me.

"Come on, they need you." She tells me while pulling me to follow her.

"What is going on Erica?"

"She is having the baby and they don't know why so early."

We went down a hallway and before we got to a room, I heard my name being screamed.

"Um, what the hell was that?"

"That would be your lovely girlfriend about to kill the doctor and nurses." She said while pushing me inside the room.

They all turned toward me when they heard the door close behind me.

"You're not supposed to be in here." The nurse said to me.

"Yes, I am, if you want her to let you do what you need to do."

I walked up to Lolo and kissed her forehead. She was sweating badly and out of breath.

"Baby, they're hurting me." She cried.

"It's going to be okay my love, I'm here," I said while holding her head to my chest.

"We need her to push now." The doctor said.

"Come on baby you can do it." I cheered her on.

She screamed and pushed at the same time. I never knew someone can scream that loud, but I guess that's only when you are pushing a baby out of you.

Once she was done pushing, she laid back against the bed taking deep breaths.

"Why can't she breathe right," I asked them, getting worried.

"She is pushing out a baby, so it's normal. She'll be fine once it's over with." The nurse tells me.

"Okay, one more big push." The doctor said.

I held her hand wishing I didn't because when she pushed, I thought she was going to break my hand in half.

After that last push, we heard a cry and London laid back on the bed with her eyes closed.

I kissed her forehead, "You did it, my love." I whispered.

"Is she okay? Why did she come so early?" She asked with her eyes still closed.

I looked at the doctor and she looked like she didn't know why either.

The nurse brought the baby over and placed her on London's chest causing her to open her eyes.

"She is beautiful." She whispered.

"You have a healthy baby girl." The nurse said.

I smiled down at them both, this is how my family is starting but I still have one more step to do.

"What will her name be?" Dr. White asked.

"Emma Sophia Wilson-Smith," London said with a big smile on her face.

I walked out of the room and told everyone they can come in now.

Emily was the first one in the room and ran up to her sister hugging her tight but making sure she didn't hurt the baby.

"You scared me, little sister." She cried.

"I scared myself, I thought I did something wrong with her."

Everyone else came in telling her how worried they were about her.

"What's her name?" Erica said.

"Emma   Sophia   Wilson-Smith.

Chapter 29

London

Once Laura told them what our baby girl's name was, Erica, stood there frozen. I thought we were going to have to get a doctor for her.

"You gave her my middle name." She said with tears.

I nodded my head. "She needed the name of her god mom and the person that kept her mom safe," I told her.

She hugged me tight and cried on my shoulder. I hugged her back and kissed the top of her head.

I didn't have Emma on her birthday, but she still will be her god mom no matter what.

While everyone was sitting around the room talking and trying to hold the baby I was starting to doze off.

Pushing out a baby is a lot of work, and I will never go through that again. Well, I didn't have a choice this time but that is the past and my baby girl is my world.

I was close to fully being asleep until the door to the room opened loud and in walked my father.

"Sorry I was at work." He said while walking over to me.

I smiled up at him and hugged him back when he hugged me.

After a while, I finally had fallen asleep.

I woke up to the sound of crying and seeing Laura singing to the baby getting her to be quiet.

"Let me feed her," I told her while sitting up in the bed.

She walked over to me and placed her in my arms, and I pulled out my breast letting her feed.

"She's beautiful just like you my love," Laura said with a big smile.

Looking down at her I couldn't do anything but smile. She looks nothing like him, and she has my eyes which I am thankful for.

It felt weird breastfeeding but after a while, I got used to it.

"I'm a little jealous now." Laura joked.

"Why is that my love?"

"She gets to suck on the breast, and I just have to sit here and watch." She said making us both laugh.

Once she was done feeding, I burped her and passed her back to Laura who just wanted to sit up and hold her.

I laid back down feeling tired still, but I didn't want to go back to sleep.

I pressed the button to call for the nurse and waited for someone to come in. I was in pain and needed something to take.

They were holding me overnight and holding Emma for two nights making sure everything was good with her since she came 2 months early.

They were surprised when nothing was wrong with her lungs, and she was able to breastfeed right away.

I knew then that my baby was a fighter, and she wasn't going to let anything keep her from being in this world.

I now know how all the parents feel when it comes down to their kids. It's love at first sight.

Once you have your baby in your arms you knew you'll do anything to make them happy and keep them safe. That's why I'm glad I killed her father.

A nurse finally came, "What can I get for you, Ms. Wilson?"

"Can I get something for this pain?"

She nodded her head and walked out and came back a few minutes later with medicine that goes into the I.V.

"This should kick in right away." She said while putting it into the I.V.

I nodded my head as I watch my girlfriend reading to Emma. With these two I can do anything.

After a few minutes of having the medicine, I started feeling high. Whatever she gave me was making me feel amazing and I was loving it.

It was the last day for Emma to be in the hospital and the doctor was taking forever to let us go.

I wanted to finally take our baby home and be in our bed.

After another 20 minutes, she finally came back in with the discharged papers and told us we were free to go.

We already had her in her car seat and wrapped up nice and tight. Laura carried her out and I had the baby bag.

We made it to the car, and I got in while Laura put the baby in the car.

After I was discharged, I never left the hospital, I wasn't going to leave the hospital without my baby girl.

She got into the car herself once the baby was in and we were off toward the house. I couldn't wait because I wanted to take a hot shower and cuddle up with my lover while our baby girl slept.

We made it home in 30 minutes because we stopped off and grabbed some food since neither of us wanted to cook.

Laura took the baby and I grabbed everything else out of the car and followed her into the house.

I walked into the kitchen and placed the food down on the table and went upstairs to help with the baby. It was like I couldn't be away from Emma or that I didn't want to be away from her.

After the baby was in the bed, we grabbed the baby monitor and headed downstairs to the kitchen. We sat there and ate.

"I'm glad to be home."

"I'm glad to have both of you home."

We finish eating and I went upstairs to our room and went into the bathroom for my shower.

I took my shower and got dressed to relax in bed with my lover. When I came out of the bathroom Laura was already in bed.

She must have taken a shower in the other bathroom when she could have joined me in mine.

I got into bed and snuggled up to her and watched whatever she had on the T.V.

"I love you," I said before kissing her lips. "I love you more."

Chapter 30

One year later:

I can't believe it's been a year since Emma was born, and Laura and I elope. We didn't want a wedding, we just wanted the ones close to us to be there, sadly Laura's parents were killed in a car crash and they were the only family that she had.

Today is my princess's birthday and we are giving her a big birthday party at her favorite park that we take her to after daycare.

We put her in daycare when she turned 4 months because I had landed a teaching job and we didn't have anyone to watch her for us.

Come to find out all the kids and parents love Emma, and she has a lot of friends to be a 1-year-old.

We took invitations up to the daycare a week ago asking them if they can pass them to the parents as they pick up their kids.

I looked over to Laura and saw that she was still sleeping I kissed her cheek and got out of bed and headed into Emma's room to find her wide awake and sucking on her thumb.

Trying to break her from that has been hard, so I gave up trying and just said she'll grow out of it.

"Good morning birthday girl," I said to her while picking her up from the bed.

I changed her and went back into our room where Laura is still sleeping.

"Looks like you gave mama a hard time last night baby girl," I said in my baby voice that always makes her laugh.

I walked over to the bed and got back into it letting her wake Laura up from her sleep.

She crawled over to her mama and started climbing on her.

"How did you get in here?" Laura asked her in a sleepy voice.

You can tell she is trying to learn to talk which I believe will happen soon because Emma is a smart kid.

We make sure to read to her every day and we don't let her watch T.V. too much. That's bad for the brain.

Laura sat up in the bed and kissed my lips and then picked up Emma kissing her all over her face and making her scream with laughter.

"Good morning princess, is someone ready for their birthday to begin?" She asked her, and it almost sounded like she said yes.

The only word Emma knows how to say is mama and that makes me a little jealous, but we come to learn that she calls us both mamas. We only know who she is talking to when she reaches for us.

We all go downstairs for breakfast which Laura cooks; she does the cooking and I do the cleaning that's how it is in this house.

I put Emma in her highchair, and I sit down next to her.

"Did everyone reply to the invitation?" She asked.

"Yes, everyone replied and will be there at 3 PM."

Emma is having a princess and prince party. It's supposed to be only a princess party but since boys are coming, I made it princess and prince. Everyone had to dress up as a princess or prince.

We talked about the party making sure we had everything and making sure we called the company that is sending the characters and bouncy house. I called the caterer yesterday making sure they had the food right and will be there on time.

I wanted her first birthday to be amazing, not only for her but for me as well.

Laura brought the food over to the table and went back and grabbed the orange juice. We ate, and I tried to feed Emma as well, but she wouldn't eat. I know it's early to feed her table food, but she likes it.

When she got like this, I knew she wanted to be fed. I stopped eating and took her out of her highchair and sat her on my lap and begin to breastfeed her.

We didn't want her on the bottle, and we said we wouldn't stop breastfeeding until she was 2 years old.

As she was feeding, I was eating and talking with my wife.

After breakfast, Laura took Emma upstairs and bathed her while I cleaned the kitchen back up which didn't take long.

Once I was done, I went upstairs and took a quick shower, and got dressed, so I can get Emma while Laura had her shower.

I looked at the clock and saw that it was only 10:30 AM and we had a little minute before it was time to leave for the park.

Emma just woke up from her nap and we are now getting her ready for her birthday party. I'm excited about this party, maybe because I never got anything like this when I was younger, and I want her to have everything she can dream of.

Since Laura and I got dressed while Emma was sleeping, we just need to finish getting her ready and leave out the door.

We need to be the first ones there, so we can make sure everything is in place and greet the guest.

I finish getting her ready while Laura grabbed everything we needed and took it to the car. I had to remind her to grab the stroller.

Finally, after getting everything together and having the princess dressed, we are now heading out of the house and toward the park.

I know it's crazy to have a party at the park where anyone could come, but that's what we want.

"Do you have everything you need?" I asked.

"Yes, all gifts in the trunk, baby bag in the backseat, and the stroller in the trunk as well." She replied while pulling out of the driveway.

We listen to music as she drove and sang along making Emma laugh. She love's listening to music.

After 20 minutes of driving, we finally made it to the park and the cater was there already setting things up.

Laura went over to speak with them while I got Emma out of the car. Once I had her out of the car, I walked over to them to make sure everything was going as planned.

"We have everything you asked for Mrs. Smith." The lady said, who name I forgot.

I nodded my head and sat at the table where all the gifts will be.

Not long after Emily and her family showed up. Abigail ran over to me and tried to grab Emma making us all laugh.

"Abbi she is almost as big as you," I said through my laughter.

I held Emma up allowing Abbi to hold her while I was still holding her.

"My baby." She said, she always called Emma her baby and I'm starting to think she thinks Emma is her baby.

"Happy birthday princess." My sister said to Emma while grabbing her from Abigail.

An hour later everyone was showing up and all the kids had on princess and prince outfits looking so damn cute.

They all started cheering when they saw the princess and prince coming. Some of the kids ran to their parents being afraid of the characters.

There was a photo booth set up for everyone to take pictures with the characters. Emma was the first one to get hers done and I was surprised she didn't cry when they held her.

I knew she wasn't going to be afraid of anything or let anything get in her way. When she put her mind to something she does it, that's how she started walking at 10 months, but I still bring the stroller with us for when she falls asleep while we're out.

The party was in full motion everything was going as planned. The kids were having an amazing time and even adults.

I was laughing hard when Erica dragged Erin into the bounce house with the kids. I swear my best friend can be a big kid at times.

I let Emma walk around to play with the other kids, but I kept an eye on her not letting her get too far from my sight.

I turned my head for a second when I heard my name being called and turned around to pay attention to Emma.

Feeling myself starting to panic when I didn't see her.

"EMMA!" I called out her name.

Laura was running over to me, "what's wrong?"

"I can't find Emma, she was right here a minute ago," I tell her before running around the park searching for her.

God this can't be happening to me, where could she be.

"Emma!"

To be continued in the next sequel, Finding Emma!

Message from the author

The purpose behind this fiction story is to let any and everyone know that there is always someone there to be by your side when you feel like the world is giving up on you.

Always remember that just because a lot of people didn't believe what happened to you, there is always that one person that will believe you, and that's all that it will take, and it will feel like the world has been lifted from your shoulders.

When something like this happens, never allow it to have a hold on you, to where you don't have trust in love, and are afraid to put yourself out there. That is only allowing them to have power over you.

Take back your power!

Made in the USA
Columbia, SC
06 July 2022